MONSTER JUICE

Fartsunami

by M. D. Payne

Grosset & Dunlap
An Imprint of Penguin Group (USA) Inc.

GROSSET & DUNLAP
Published by the Penguin Group
Penguin Group (USA) Inc., 375 Hudson Street, New York, New York 10014, USA

USA | Canada | UK | Ireland | Australia | New Zealand | India | South Africa | China
Penguin Books Ltd, Registered Offices: 80 Strand, London WC2R 0RL, England

For more information about the Penguin Group visit penguin.com

Cover illustrated by Amanda Dockery

Library of Congress Cataloging-in-Publication Data is available.

ISBN 978-0-448-46227-1 10 9 8 7 6 5 4 3 2 1

To Major Payne and Mummy,
for all their love and farts

Prologue

The fat man in the suit fell to the floor, writhing and drooling.

"Der Schmerz!" he moaned in his native tongue. *"Nein! Ich kann es nicht kämpfen . . ."*

His assistants—even larger, almost identical men—rushed into the man's office. They were dressed in casual tropical clothes.

He kicked wildly as he fought his invisible attacker. His huge figure shimmied and shook. He knocked over a lamp that smashed into his aquarium, spilling piranhas onto the plush carpet. They flopped around wildly, splashing in the thin layer of water that was left. The fish bounced over to the writhing man, and bit his twitching body.

CRUNCH. CRUNCH. CRUNCH.

But the crunch wasn't the sound of the man's flesh—it was the sound of the piranhas' teeth shattering!

The assistants kicked the piranhas off of their boss and bent down to help him up. Sweat poured down his contorted face.

"Aaaaaahhhhhhhh!" he moaned.

It was hot in the room—as if the air-conditioning had failed.

"The window," said one of his assistants, "is open."

"Close it," said the other. "Now!"

He jumped up to do so, when a large sucking noise stopped him in his tracks.

The sound came from the man.

SLLLLLLUUUUUUUUUUUUPPPPPPPPPPP!

The suited man twitched a few more times . . .

SLLLLUUUUUPPP!

Gave one final yawp . . .

ZLIP!

And then he farted an intensely long, loud fart. After it stopped, he coughed violently, and then passed out, his head bonking onto the floor.

The two assistants quickly moved to cover their noses and waited for a great stench.

It never came.

The suited man snored with a look of contentment on his face.

The two assistants stared at each other, not sure what to do.

The one near the window slammed it down forcefully, locking out the hot, salty air.

Then, both assistants carefully picked up their boss and brought him to the infirmary.

Once he was placed on the table, the ancient witch doctor looked him over carefully from head to toe. He burned incense. He applied jungle leeches. He mumbled spells. He shook his staff angrily.

The boss-man's assistants wrung their hands, not knowing how to help.

"Is he okay?" asked one.

"Do you know what's happened to him?" asked the other.

The witch doctor scratched his head.

"A thing like this, I have never seen," he said in a deep and otherworldly voice. "He seems normal—healthy, even—but, alas, my leeches cannot dine upon his blood." He lifted one of the slimy black slugs to his ear. "They say that it's as if something has enveloped his body, but I see nothing. Very, very distressed I am. I will raise a few spirits tonight to see what they have to say about this."

"What can we do?" one assistant asked.

"Rest, he must," said the witch doctor. "Take him to his bed and keep your eyes on him."

The two assistants carried out the witch doctor's orders. Despite the fact that neither leeches nor piranhas could make a mark on their boss's skin, they made sure to close his netting. No vampire mosquitoes or zombie frogs could dine on him in the night.

They stood watch, but all their boss did was snore, and occasionally giggle. Outside, the jungle seethed with the sound of mysterious creatures.

In the morning, as the first light crept in through the window, their boss awoke, refreshed and renewed.

"Gentlemen," he chortled with glee. "Vhy are you in my bedroom? Are you afraid ze mermaids vill call you out to sea again?"

"Boss," one asked, "don't you remember what happened last night?"

"Vell," he said as he scratched his head, "I vas reading ze latest numbers on ze residents' lebensplasm . . ."

"And?" the other assistant asked, leaning in.

"Vell . . ." the boss said, "I can't remember. Ze next sing I do remember is vaking up here."

"How do you feel?" asked one assistant.

"Amazing!" he said. "Und I've had ze most vonderful idea!"

"What's that?" they asked in unison.

He jumped out of bed, his suit still perfectly crisp,

his leather shoes shining. The room shook and his huge jowls jiggled as he landed on the floor.

"I haff to make a very important phone call," he said.

"Boss?"

"BOSS!?!"

But, in a flash, the boss had swung the door open and run down the hall.

Dirty Work

My friends and I survived another very long day of helping out at Raven Hill Retirement Home. I sluggishly pushed my way past a few residents and out of the Great Room. Shane, Ben, and Gordon stumbled out after me. We had just cleaned up after a huge—and messy—Sunday dinner.

"It's really, really hard to feed the old monsters now that they're stronger," I said.

"Nobody got bit today, did they?" asked Ben.

"The Nurses are definitely getting bit more often," I said as we stopped in front of a room of zombies who refused to go upstairs to bed.

"Why don't the Nurses ever become monsters?" asked Gordon.

We all shrugged, too tired to care.

Three identical Nurses—huge, bulky gentlemen in one-size-too-small uniforms—struggled to get the residents out of the room and upstairs to bed.

"Hey!" one of the Nurses yelled as a wrinkled old zombie knocked him over.

The zombie playfully chewed on the small hat perched on top of the Nurse's swollen, red head. The other old zombies giggled.

"Not funny!" warned the Nurse, who jumped back up to his feet with a THUD.

The three Nurses were finally able to wrangle the residents out of the room and past us.

Once the zombies were out of the way, we shuffled past the room of old witches, who were, as always, cackling away over a special bedtime brew. We dragged our tired legs down the hallway, over the holey, moth-eaten rug.

"I was wondering how the holes got so huge," Ben said, and pointed at a figure hidden in the alcove.

Shane smiled and waved at the figure.

Moth Man, cheerily picking carpet fibers from his blackened, slimy teeth, waved back.

"Hurry up and eat the dusty old thing," said Ben. "It's giving me allergies!"

We slunk into the lobby and past the portrait of Lucinda B. Smythe. Even she looked happy tonight as she watched us walk past.

Everyone was happy at Raven Hill. Everyone but us.

"I think I might be officially done with Raven Hill," huffed Gordon. "This has stopped being a good time."

"I feel like they don't need our help anymore," I said as I opened the door and headed for freedom.

"Oh, but I can assure you that they do, Mr. Taylor," came a voice from behind us that stopped us in our tracks.

We turned. Director Z, the man in charge of Raven Hill, stood in the center of the foyer with his hands behind his back. His crisp and perfectly pressed suit gleamed from the dull light of the old, cobwebby chandelier above him. He took a few steps toward us.

"If it weren't for you gentlemen," Director Z said, "this facility and its residents would most certainly have been obliterated from the face of the Earth."

"Well, thanks for reminding us," said Gordon as he turned back to the door. "Those were some great times. Some real roach-killin' times. But, I've got practice at five a.m., and I need to get some sleep."

Gordon slipped out into the cold December air and slammed the door behind him. The creaky old house shook for a few seconds.

"If the rest of you gentlemen could spare just one

more moment," Director Z pleaded, "there's a lot to take care of before you leave for your big trip."

"Director Z!" I pleaded back. "We're exhausted! We've been here all day. We've been working so hard."

"And that is precisely the reason that everyone is doing so well!" he said. He paused for a moment and looked me straight in the eye. "Those poor old souls need you. I really wish you weren't leaving on Tuesday."

"Allll riiiight," I said, caving in once again. "What is it?"

He brought his hands out from behind his back.

He held a plunger, liquid clog remover, and a shiny metallic bag.

"We really need your help with the werewolves' bathroom," he said.

"Yeah, maybe I have practice, too," said Ben. "I'm not sure if I can smell that much wet dog without barfing."

I looked at Shane. He nodded. Ben headed home.

"All right, we're on it," I said.

Can you believe this?" I hissed as we entered the werewolves' room. "They're totally taking advantage of us! After *we* saved them from the sussuroblats, they should be waiting on us!"

"Oh come on, they're just a bunch of helpless old people," said Shane. "Remember what kind of mess this place was before we got here."

"They seem strong enough to be on their own," I said. "I mean, what did they do before we came along?"

"Before we got here, bugs were guzzling their juices . . . and who knows what's out there now, just waiting to suck it all up," Shane said.

"Well, they're gonna have to get along without us," I said. "I don't care if Director Z begs and pleads for us to stay, I'm not missing the science-class field trip. Not for *anything*."

"Ah, sunny Florida," Shane said with a smile. "A little sun. Palm trees. Sand between my toes. Florida's still really warm this time of year."

"Dude!" I yelled, "This isn't spring break. We're not going to waste our time on the beach! This trip is all about Kennedy Space Center. The astronaut training program. Getting to *touch* a moon rock. Meeting a real-life astronaut! The only sun I get will be on the Gemini launchpad. I'm soaking up every bit of cosmic information I can."

"But my mom just bought me new swim trunks," Shane added as I stormed into the bathroom. "They have surfing sharks on them."

This Could Get Hairy

Ben was right. The room smelled like wet dog. The funkiest, moldiest wet dog ever. There were other smells too, but I didn't want to think about where they'd come from.

"Next time, I'm not giving them any extra doggie treats," Shane grumbled.

Every surface was covered in hair. On the sink. On the floor. In the bathtub. Probably the ceiling, too. I didn't dare look up. The worst of all was the toilet. It was completely clogged. Wads of hair and shaving cream floated in the gloopy water. A razor and a bottle of shaving cream sat on the rim of the toilet. Both were completely covered in hair.

"Wow," I said, "I guess they shave with toilet water."

Shane peeked into the sink. "Nope," he said. "They clogged the sink, too. I guess they just switched to the toilet after that, those dirty dogs."

"I'll never figure out why they bother to shave," I said. "I mean, it's gonna grow back!"

"I think they like to look fresh for the ladies," said Shane. "Pietro told me he had the hots for Clarice, the banshee."

"A werewolf and a banshee?" I asked. "Can they do that?"

Shane turned from the sink. "Who are you to say that two people—or geriatric monsters—can't fall in love?"

"You have a point, but we should still show Clarice this bathroom and save her some trouble," I snickered.

Shane shook his head. "Where should we start?" he asked.

After cleaning the hair off the floor and around the sink, we stuffed it all in the bag that the Director had given us. It was going pretty quickly.

Then we started on the toilet.

Shane was plunging like a madman as the moon rose and shone through the bathroom window.

"I think I'm getting it," he said. "The water's going down!"

"Dude," I said. "That's only because you're getting it all over our shoes."

"Ugh!" he yelled.

He let the plunger go.

But it kept plunging.

"Huh?" Shane gasped, and he turned to me.

It bounced and splashed around, and a growling sound bubbled up from the toilet.

Gurrble, Grrrble, Burrbble!

"Grab the plunger!" I screamed. "Plunge whatever it is out of here."

Shane and I grasped for the handle, but I couldn't hang on. It bounced around and . . .

FWACK!

The handle hit me right on the head. I stumbled back and hit the cold tiles with an *"OOF."*

Shane still had a good grip. He plunged with all his might. Pulling back, the plunger came out of the toilet with a FLOOP. Shane hit the floor, butt-first, right next to me.

"Is the water going down?" I croaked.

"Let me see," Shane said. He fumbled back up on his feet, and peered into the toilet.

The toilet started to shake and vibrate.

GURRRBLE, GRRRRR, BURRBBLE!

"I can't tell if the water is going down, but something is definitely coming up!" he said, and started to back away from the bowl.

Before we could skitter out of the room, the toilet

exploded all over Shane. He was completely covered in wet brown goo.

He turned to me, his eyes squeezed shut, and said, while trying to keep his mouth closed, "Please tell me this isn't what I think it is."

"Most of it isn't," I replied, trying to sound encouraging.

Shane stood frozen in disgust as the brown goo dripped down his body and piled up on his feet.

It formed the largest, nastiest wad of goopy hair I'd ever laid eyes on.

"Open your eyes," I said. "You have to see this."

"What!?" Shane yelled as he pried open his eyes.

We stared at the wet werewolf hair wad growing on the floor.

"Well, this is something new," he said. "It's a furwad!"

"Hairwad," I insisted. "Unless they were shaving in werewolf form."

"Are you sure," Shane continued. "I think—"

The hairwad shook violently and growled a low, angry growl.

"Forget it! The liquid clog remover!" I yelled.

Shane bent over quick, grabbed the liquid clog remover, and poured it all over the hairwad.

There was a whimper and squeal as the hair broke up and got sucked down the drain on the floor.

"Whew!" I said, and high-fived Shane. "Well done, man!"

That's when we noticed something crawling out of the sink.

"GRRRRRRRR!"

"Um, Shane?" I asked, "Did you happen to save any of that clog remover?"

"Sadly," said Shane, "no."

The hairwad slowly crept out of the sink. It flopped onto the cold, hard bathroom floor. It headed toward us, leaving behind a slimy, watery trail.

"Any bright ideas?" asked Shane.

"Um . . . uh . . ." My brain froze as the hairwad inched closer, growling all the way.

And then the hairwad pounced. It jumped amazingly high—right toward my face.

"Ah!" I yelled, and grabbed the hairwad.

It writhed and spat and growled. It smelled terrible. I couldn't see any claws, teeth, or even a mouth, but I had little doubt that it could hurt me. I struggled to hold it as far away from my face as possible.

"Hold on!" said Shane, and he waved the mysterious metallic bag in front of me. "Can you get it in here? It doesn't seem like the hair we put in earlier is doing anything."

I looked through the bathroom window and saw the moon. Suddenly everything clicked.

"Of course," I yelled. "The hair is freaking out because of the moon. This must be a silver bag. It blocks moon rays!"

"Thanks for the mad-science lesson," Shane said as he tried to position the bag under the struggling hairwad.

As I pushed the hair down toward the bag, it started whimpering like a puppy.

"Don't listen to it!" yelled Shane.

I forced the quivering, growling hair in the bag. It began to shake violently and . . .

SILENCE.

Shane quickly tied up the bag and glanced over to the sink. It was empty.

"The hair must have unclogged itself," Shane said.

"It's about time the monsters cleaned up after themselves," I snickered.

"Speaking of cleaning up," Shane said, "I'm desperate for a shower."

We headed out of Raven Hill, and the smell of wet werewolf, and worse, followed us all the way home.

We Gotta Get Outta This Place

"Can you believe Director Z made us clean the werewolf bathroom?" I groaned as I poked at the Mac 'n' Sneeze on my plate.

"You're forgetting to speak in code," said Ben, peering nervously around the cafeteria.

"Oh right," I said, lowering my voice a little. "Can you believe *the guy* who runs *the place* at the *top of the hill* made us clean *the place* where *the hairy dog men* go *potty*?"

"Yes," said Gordon, "I can believe it. That's why I left."

"How *was* practice?" Shane asked Gordon.

"Just like the Mac 'n' Sneeze today," said Gordon. "TERRIBLE."

"Yeah, it does taste a little funky," agreed Shane. "Almost fishy."

Gordon stretched his neck and his bones cracked.

"I just couldn't loosen up," he continued. "I felt like a zombie."

"Billy and the other zombies might disagree," Ben said, "but I totally know what you mean."

"Dude, the code," I mocked Ben.

"Arrggh," Ben said, "You're right. *Random* zombies might disagree."

"Maybe we should just stop saying the word 'zombie.'" said Shane. "Oh, wait. I said it again."

"Where were you this morning?" I asked Shane. "I texted you twenty times! You were supposed to help me figure out our itinerary for Kennedy Space Center. We have to make sure we can see everything. There's a lot of stuff to do, and we're only there for a week, and we already have one whole day filled with astronaut training, and—"

"Yawn," said Gordon, which made Ben yawn. "Boooooring."

"Yawn!?" I screeched. "Guys, this is the closest we'll ever get to space! Aren't you excited?"

"Actually," said Gordon, "this is the closest we'll get to Cocoa Beach—home of Ron Jon Surf Shop. Do you think Mr. Stewart will take us?"

"Since when are you a surfer?" I asked.

"I keep up on all sports, even the extreme ones," Gordon said with a smile.

"I know Shane's excited about getting some sun," I said. "What about you, Ben?"

"I'm just worried about barfing on the plane. This is the first time I've ever flown anywhere. Speaking of barf, did the hairwads from *the hairy dog men* smell?" asked Ben. "I bet they smelled."

"Terribly!" I gagged. "You were right—you wouldn't have been able to make it very long without spewing."

"At least it wasn't as bad as *the fishy old man from the swamp's* gas," Shane said. "I wonder what his bathroom looks like these days."

"Who?" asked Gordon.

"Gil," whispered Shane.

"The cooooooooode," whispered Ben, even more quietly.

"Yeah, his farts are insanely nasty," I said. "That was a great idea you had to just cork his butt, Ben. Which reminds me—where is the cork?"

"I think it's still in my bag," Shane said. "But that doesn't mean it's my turn to plug him up. It's definitely your turn next time. The last time my thumb slipped and—"

"AHEM!"

The "AHEM" came from behind me, and I turned around to see . . .

THE LUNCH LADY.

Ben choked on his Mac 'n' Sneeze. Shane and Gordon both looked in different directions.

Lunch Lady and I locked eyes.

She had only spoken to me once before—at Raven Hill, after my friends and I saved the old monsters there from the disgusting cat-size cockroach creatures known as sussuroblats. They had been draining the monsters of their lebensplasm, as Director Z liked to call it—or "monster juice," as we liked to call it.

She had surprised me with the news that she worked with Director Z and his Nurses to keep an eye on the kids at Rio Vista Middle School. When she found a kid that might be able to help out at the home, she whipped up a special bit of food that, once eaten, led them to Raven Hill.

So far, I'm the only person who's ever gotten to taste her Raven Hill recipes.

"May I have a word weeth you?" she asked.

"Aren't you . . . ?" I looked over at the line of students waiting at the hot-lunch counter.

"Busy?" she finished my sentence. "Not at all."

A Nurse—not the school nurse, but one of the Nurses from Raven Hill—slid into place behind the hot-lunch counter. His big beefy arms were better at detaining demented monsters than doling out scoops of food. He was practically cracking the platters as he brought the scooper down.

"Come weeth me," she said.

We walked out of the cafeteria and into the hall. I didn't say anything, and just let Lunch Lady lead me down the math and science wing, straight into . . .

"Mr. Stewart's office?" I asked.

We stood in the middle of my chemistry teacher's room.

"Does he work for Raven Hill, too?" I asked.

"No," said Lunch Lady. "But the laboratory in the back is soundproof, and that's where he spends his entire lunch. So we won't be heard here."

"Oh," I said, a little disappointed.

She shut the door and glared at me.

"What are you gentlemen do-eeng?" she asked. "Are you out of your minds?"

"I'm sorry, I—" I started to say.

"Don't know what you mean?" she finished my sentence . . . again. "Yes, well, that's thee problem. You guys don't even realize how much you've been blabbing about Raven Heell. You're acting like workeeng een a retirement home for monsters iss perfectly normal. I just heard you talkeeng about werewolf hair theengies . . ."

"Hairwads," I interrupted her this time.

". . . all the way over at my counter. What iff students started leesteneeeng een to your conversations?"

"So what?" I said, suddenly angry. "They'll just think we're talking about some crazy video game. We need to get this stuff off of our chest—Director Z and the Nurses have been working us way too hard. We don't even know what we're saying anymore!" I knew I was whining, but I couldn't help it. "When we agreed to help out at Raven Hill, we all thought it would be an adventure. We thought we'd get to know more about the monsters, maybe learn more about their secret powers. It was awesome when we were battling evil cockroaches together. Now it feels like they're just using us to cook and clean—while they get stronger and angrier."

"Yeah, well, you better keep your tongue at school, or I might feed you sometheeng that will make you mute," she said, wagging a finger at me.

"Fine," I said. "But since you're spying on me, tell Director Z that once we're gone, he'll see that the monsters can take care of themselves."

The bell rang, and lunch was over.

Lunch Lady opened up Mr. Stewart's door and headed back to the cafeteria. I followed her.

She was right. We *were* talking about Raven Hill constantly. But it was hard not to. They were just driving us crazy—and it would *never* be anything but crazy at Raven Hill. I desperately needed a break from the madness, the sleepless nights, the annoying grunts and moans.

I returned to my friends and my Mac 'n' Sneeze.

"I wish we were leaving for the trip right now," I said, and laid my head on the table.

Strange Visitors

That night, as usual, we slowly rode our bikes up the windy, overgrown road to the top of Raven Hill.

The ravens circled above us. One cawed.

"It's nice to see you again, too, Balfor," I said.

"Don't lie to the nice raven," said Shane.

Balfor landed on the nest on the tallest spire of Raven Hill and cocked his head strangely. "What is it?" I asked Balfor, and turned around.

Speeding up the hill was a man in a crisp, pressed suit very much like Director Z's. But unlike the skinny and gaunt Director Z, this gentleman was plump with a well-tanned face. His huge mustache bristled as he approached us. He stormed right up to me, grabbed me by my jacket, and pulled me up so fast that I lost my breath.

"Hey!" I squeaked.

His face turned from deep tan to red.

"Vhat are you kids doing up here? Spying on zese poor old folks?" he demanded.

"No," I pleaded, trying to shake free of his swollen hands. "We're here to help."

"What are *we* doing?" Gordon yelled as he jumped up to grab me. "What are *you* doing? Who are you? Put him down!"

The plump man ignored Gordon and turned around to yell down the road, "Vell, vould you hurry it up! Ve seem to be haffing an issue here!"

Two identical figures lumbered up the side of the hill. They were huge—the ground shook as they huffed and puffed their way up to where we stood.

"Wait," Shane said. "Those guys look like Nurses!"

They were Nurses, although strangely, they didn't have on the usual white Nurses' uniforms. These two wore Bermuda shorts and colorful Hawaiian shirts.

Shane ran down to meet them.

"Hey, guys! Can you help us with this maniac?!" Shane yelled.

The two Nurses charged up to Shane—and pushed him into the dirt!

"This is crazy!" yelled Ben, and he ran into the retirement home to get help.

Shane jumped up and assumed a karate fighting position, but the Nurses had already passed him by. They easily dragged Gordon off me, and then yanked me from the hands of the plump man.

The well-dressed gentleman loomed over us and cracked his chunky knuckles.

"I vill ask you again," he said. "Vhat are you kids doing up here?"

Shane yelled as he reached us, "Don't you dare hurt them."

He paused nervously in front of the gentleman, not quite sure what to do.

Gordon and I squirmed, but the Tropical Nurses were strong. We weren't going anywhere.

"Who are you?" Shane demanded.

The mustached gentleman eyed us with caution and said, slowly, "I'm ze Direktor."

He leaned in closer to me. I could smell his breath as he said, "And I vant to know vhat you're up to here."

Shane ran at the Direktor, when . . .

"GENTLEMEN!"

A booming voice from the retirement home stopped everyone.

We looked up to see Director Z calmly walking down the stairs, followed by a twitchy Ben.

"I believe there's been a huge misunderstanding," Director Z said calmly.

He walked toward us and stuck out his hand.

"Herr Direktor Detlef, it's been quite a long time," he said.

"Director Zachary!" he yelled back. "It's quite good to see you!"

He grabbed Director Z and hugged him so hard that we heard bones snap.

"Yes, quite good," said Director Z, rubbing his side with a grimace. "Now, what seems to be the trouble with my associates?"

"*Your* associates?" Herr Direktor Detlef gasped. "Oh, zese must be ze *children* zat saved your facility—of course."

He waved at the Tropical Nurses to let Gordon and me go. Shane stood down.

"I'm so very sorry," Herr Direktor Detlef said.

He and the Tropical Nurses gave each of us a hand-crushing handshake as we introduced ourselves.

"Here I vas sinking you were spying on ze facility." He laughed. "And it is you who have saved it. Vait until I tell everyone at ze facility back home."

"My pleasure," I said, as I cradled my crushed hand.

"Well, then," Director Z said, "we don't have any more time for introductions, as I've gathered all the residents for a briefing, and they grow weary. What took you so long, Herr Direktor?"

"Ve parked at ze bottom of ze hill," he responded. "I alvays like to get a little bit of exercise ven I can.

He pat his large belly as if it was a beautifully sculpted set of abs.

Ben fired off a series of questions: "Facility back home? Briefing? What's going on?"

"All will be explained inside," insisted Director Z.

We stepped into the foyer, and almost immediately, the painting of Lucinda B. Smythe began to scream at Herr Direktor Detlef.

"You charlatan. Leave this house at once!" Lucinda yelled from her dusty frame.

"Lucinda, dear," scolded Director Z, "you mustn't treat our guest so rudely. He's come too far to suffer your wicked tongue-lashing. I do apologize, Herr Direktor, but Lucinda has quite a rude streak in her."

"That's all right, Zachary," said Herr Direktor Detlef. "I've heard worse from some of my residents."

"No, it's not *all right*," screamed Lucinda. "This isn't *all right* at all. Get this *thing* out of my house!"

"We don't have time to quibble, Lucinda," said Director Z as he walked by the cranky portrait. "We've got business to attend to in the Great Room."

Excuse Me

The Great Room was packed. Rows of old monsters lined up from front to back and side to side. They whispered and growled excitedly—a change from their normal moaning and groaning. I rubbed my sore body.

Director Z pointed to a couple of empty seats in the back row.

"Gentlemen," he said to us, "we've saved you these seats. Please take them quickly, as we must get started."

He and Herr Direktor Detlef rushed up to the front of the room as we sat down. Horace, the old organ player, tapped out a more upbeat tune than usual on his keyboard. The tune made Herr Direktor Detlef smile, and he began to say something to Director Z, who laughed.

Shane and I leaned in to hear what they were saying. That's when Shane noticed whose behind we were sitting behind.

"Oh no . . ." Shane said and pointed in front of him.

It was Gil, the creature from the swamp.

"Oh man," said Ben, "I think I'm going to hurl."

"What was on the menu?" Gordon asked. "You know . . . what did he eat for lunch?"

"It's Monday," I said. "So . . ."

"Mexican fiesta," we all said at once.

We didn't have any time to move.

"Ladies and gentlemen," Director Z started, "I have a very special guest to introduce to you tonight, and he comes with some very exciting news—Herr Direktor Detlef from the Paradise Retirement Island in the Bermuda Triangle."

Herr Direktor Detlef stood up. The crowd applauded loudly. Then Horace stopped the organ music and everyone stared, waiting for the Direktor to speak. Mouths opened in anticipation. A wad of drool escaped from one of the zombies' mouths and hit the floor with a PLOP.

"Ladies und gentlemen!" boomed the Direktor. "I come to Raven Hill bearing news of great significance. Ve heard vhat you vent through vith sose terrible sussuroblats. Ve, too, vere once veak and now haff gained strength."

PFFFFTTT!

"Oh, sheesh!" whispered Ben. "He's starting."

Sure enough, a small green cloud of gas wafted up from the wrinkled and scaly green bottom of the swamp creature.

Herr Direktor Detlef continued, unaware of the swamp gas. "Sussuroblats haff a very hard time swimming. So, ve veren't nearly as veakened as you vere, and can only imagine how hard it vas to be at ze epicenter of ze attack . . ."

PPFFFFFFTTTTTTT!

A larger cloud floated up from the swamp creature's seat. He sat happily in the cloud before it slowly drifted back toward us. The four of us blew as hard as we could and pushed it toward the front of the room. This time, a few of the residents started coughing.

"His swamp gas is outta control!" hissed Gordon.

"Hold on," said Shane, rummaging around in his bag, "let me get the cork . . ."

Shane pulled out the prized cork, and handed it to me.

"You're closest," he said. "Do the deed."

"But you're better at it!" I said while handing it back. "Just do it."

"Rock Paper Scissors?" asked Shane.

"You're on!" I said.

PFFFTTTTTSS!

"Make it quick," said Ben, who had taken on a greenish hue. "I can't take much more."

Herr Direktor Detlef kept talking, but we were too busy to notice what he said.

"One, two, three!"

I had rock. Shane had paper.

"NOOO!" I hissed, and snatched the cork out of Shane's hand. "He's sitting down. What am I supposed to do?"

Ben grabbed his cell phone and flung it under the swamp creature's chair. It landed next to his webbed foot.

"Huh?" said the swamp creature. He bent over awkwardly to grab the cell phone. I cautiously leaned forward and through my watering eyes I searched for my target. And there it was, between his frizzled green buttocks. I held my breath and started to make my move.

I hadn't quite finished when the swamp creature shuffled around and stared at me with a puzzled look on his face. I jerked my hands back to the top of his seat and gripped it nervously.

"Uhhhh . . . ," I stuttered.

"Is this crazy contraption one of yours?" he asked while holding up the phone.

"It's mine," Ben replied, grabbing his phone. "Sorry."

The swamp creature turned his attention back to the stage and slowly started to lower his backside onto the seat. I quickly tried to finish the deed.

SHHHHHRRRRPPPP

A little gas seeped out from around the cork, I could feel it like a warm breeze on my hand.

"Get out of there," Shane whispered.

"I haven't pushed it in far enough yet," I whispered back.

My hand would soon be sandwiched between his posterior and the seat.

"Oops!" Ben yelled, and dropped the phone under the swamp creature's chair again.

"You brainless buffoons," the swamp creature muttered.

The phone had slid a little farther forward this time, and the swamp creature had to hold on to the chair in front of him in order to bend over far enough to grab it. Soon, we were cheek to cheek. Well . . . butt-cheek to cheek. Not wanting to get my hands too far into a swamp butt, I grabbed my cell phone and used it to prod the cork tightly into place.

"I'm going to need to boil this before I can use it again," I said.

The swamp creature sat down and Herr Direktor Detlef rambled on.

"It really is quite amazing vhat has happened here at Raven Hill," the Direktor continued. "Ze energy gained by ze network of retirement homes is invaluable. Giff yourself a round of applause!"

The Great Room filled with applause, hoots, and cheers. The zombies moaned happily, the werewolves howled, and the witches cackled with glee.

The swamp creature stood up to applaud with the rest of the monsters.

The Direktor boomed above the applause: "Zat said, it's my distinct pleasure to announce—"

He was interrupted by a great rumble from the swamp creature.

BLLLLLUUUUUURRRRRGGGGG!

"Uh-oh," said Ben.

Our chairs vibrated. Above us, a crystal chandelier dropped wisps of spiderweb as it started to sway.

"Oh no!" Gordon gulped. "I don't think the cork is going to hold."

Before we could do anything, the excited swamp creature let out the most rip-roaring raunch *ever*. The cork flew out of his fishy old butt and hit me right between the eyes. I stumbled back into my chair. Stars danced before my eyes. I stood up and tried to get out of the way, but it was no use. The green cloud surrounded me.

"We're going to need a bigger cork," Shane announced as the room turned black and I tumbled to the floor.

My last thought was *I wish I had left for Kennedy Space Center today . . .*

Three, Two, One, LIFTOFF!

At lunch the next day, we spoke about normal, non-monstery things for once.

"No, really," said Gordon, "I think that we have a really good chance at making regionals this year."

"Yeah, right," said Shane. "I'll wager you a Grilled Screams that you guys win three games—TOPS."

"We just need practice and focus!" Gordon said, "I even convinced Coach Grey to come along on the science trip so we can practice. Everyone on the team is already going to be there. Plus, all the pros train in Florida."

"Hey, are you guys practicing on Cocoa Beach, perchance?" asked Shane.

"Guys," I said, almost choking on a Chicken Linger,

"can you please just *pretend* to be excited about touching a moon rock? Or seeing a Space Shuttle?"

"I'll be excited once I survive the plane trip," said Ben as he poked at his lunch.

"We're going to have a great time at Kennedy Space Center," said Shane, "but thinking of the beach keeps me calm . . . especially when toilets explode in my face."

"Or swamp butts," Ben added.

"Look," said Gordon, "I have sports. You have space. Why do you need me to like what you like? You don't like sports, and that's fine."

"Fine," I said. "Got it. But let's not talk about monsters—the whole trip."

"Agreed," everyone said.

After lunch, almost one hundred sixth graders hovered over their luggage in the school gym, discussing how they would survive the plane ride and how much candy they had hidden in their carry-on bags. The room buzzed with anticipation.

Shane, Gordon, Ben, and I formed a tight circle.

"Wait—are there only two seats between the aisle and window, or three?" Ben asked. "If it's three, please don't make me sit alone. I hate barfing alone."

"Actually," said Gordon, while he pinched his nose and waved his hand in the air, "maybe that's why you *should* sit alone."

Gordon giggled.

"Hey!" said Ben. "I didn't make fun of you when you had a roach mouth, did I?"

"Technically, you won't be alone," said Shane. "I'm sure someone will sit next to you."

A voice from outside the circle said, "I'll sit next to you!"

"Huh?" we all said, looking around to see where it came from.

A short girl with dark hair and dark eyes walked over to our circle. She had on the thickest glasses I'd ever seen, and a fanny pack.

"I'm Nabila," she said with a grin that revealed a tangle of braces.

"Na . . . leeba?" asked Gordon.

"No, na-BE-lah," she said. "And I'd be happy to sit next to you, Ben. In fact, it would be my pleasure."

Ben looked shocked.

"Wait," I said. "Who are you? I haven't even seen you around school."

"Are you new?" asked Ben.

"Somewhat. I usually keep to myself," she said. "My family moved from Egypt this year. My dad works for the government and got transferred here."

"Sounds cool," said Shane.

"I've seen you boys around school," she said, with a smirk. "In fact, we met at Jackson Amusement Park. I was the girl at the front of the line you cut to get on the Gravitron. It took me days to get the vomit out of my hair."

"Look," I said, "thank you for saying you'd sit with Ben, but we've got him covered. Right, guys?"

"Wait a minute," said Ben. "You're more than welcome to sit next to me."

Ben bowed awkwardly.

Shane, for perhaps the first time in his life, was speechless.

Why was this nerdy girl trying to invade our group? I couldn't let this happen. I had just spent months working my tail off with my friends at Raven Hill, and I just wanted to spend a relaxing week with them at Kennedy Space Center. I didn't want an outsider coming in and ruining our fun—especially not a *girl* that Ben was flirting with.

I started to say, "Now, just wait a minute . . ."

"LADIES AND GENTLEMEN!" boomed a voice from the front of the gym.

I looked up to see Mr. Stewart holding a bullhorn.

"LET ME JUST INTRODUCE YOU TO YOUR CHAPERONES. COACH GREY . . ."

"Yeaaaaaahhhhh!" screamed all of the jocks, including Gordon.

"AND MS. VERACRUZ."

"Who's that?" I asked Ben.

"Dunno," said Ben.

We craned our necks to see where Mr. Stewart was pointing. An extremely familiar hairnet rose above some of the shorter sixth graders.

"Lunch Lady?" asked Shane.

The room spun. My stomach sank. *This can't be happening,* I thought.

"I *knew* I wouldn't get one moment's peace from Raven Hill," I said. "Lunch Lady is going to be watching our every move. Ugh!"

"Who cares?" said Ben. "We're not talking about monsters during the trip. What is she going to tell Director Z?"

I wasn't sure, but I had a really, really bad feeling. . . .

"LADIES AND GENTLEMEN, THE BUSES TO THE AIRPORT ARE OUT FRONT. PLEASE LINE UP AND GET READY TO GET GOING!"

Nabila sat next to Ben the whole bus ride to the airport. He was too shy to speak with her, so she just sat quietly watching him. When we finally got on the plane, she followed him on, and sat down right next to him.

Shane and Gordon sat in two empty seats behind them, so I was forced to sit next to her. Immediately, I went to work figuring out how to get her as far away from us as possible.

We were dealing with a new breed of monster.

Intruder Alert!

The flight down to Florida was a bumpy one.

I looked over to Ben and—big surprise—his face had gone green. His hands gripped the armrests for dear life. He was going to blow chunks any second. This could be the break I was looking for. If he lost his cookies all over Nabila, she'd surely ditch him. I didn't even care if I caught a little side splatter. It would totally be worth it.

Ben's chest started to spasm. He was going to erupt soon. Nabila just kept smiling at him. I didn't want her to think I was actually paying attention to them, so I ignored Ben's retching and went back to updating my itinerary for the space center.

Sure enough, a few bumps later, Ben was done.

WHAAAARRRFFFF!

All the kids on the plane started EWWWWWing at the top of their lungs. All but one.

Nabila wasn't EWWWWWWing.

Nabila was almost AWWWWing in amazement. She looked at Ben as if he was the most stunning thing on the planet.

She reached into her backpack and pulled out a jar. She handed it to Ben.

"Here, go in this," she said calmly and patted him on the back.

"No," he drooled. "I'm good. I think I'm okay."

Nabila yelled, "Brussels sprouts!"

WHAAAARRRRRFFFF!

And Ben threw up again.

The whole plane EEEWWWWed again—this time some of the adults joined in.

"Thanks," she said, and screwed a cap on the newly-filled jar.

I watched the whole thing in amazement, trying my best to ignore Nabila, but I just couldn't.

"What are you DOING?" I screeched.

"Collecting a sample," she said. "As far as we know, Ben's vomit is the only non-sussuroblat vomit that can actually melt a sussuroblat. It needs to be studied."

"WHAT!?" both Ben and I yelped.

"How do you know what a sussuroblat is?" I demanded.

"You guys talk about *everything* at lunch," she said. "I heard about sussuroblats from you."

Ben and I gasped.

Shane and Gordon popped up from their seats behind us.

"WHAT?!" they both yelped.

"I knew that those roaches you led into the Gravitron were not ordinary roaches. I knew something else was going on. So, the next week at school, I started listening in on your lunchtime conversations. Now that I know you're helping defend a bunch of old monsters from some force of evil," she said matter-of-factly. "I want in."

"In?" I asked. "In on what?"

"On the action," she said. "I want to help you guys out. Most of all, I want to meet the monsters."

We were stunned.

Before we could even ask why, Lunch Lady appeared out of nowhere. I almost jumped out of my skin!

"What eeesss going on here?" she asked.

I stammered to get out a reply when Nabila said simply, "Ben threw up."

"All right," she said, eyeing me suspiciously. "I'll geet a flight attendant."

She turned to leave, and we all stared at Nabila again.

"Yes," she said, "I know she's part of Raven Hill, too. And I'm not about to let her know I heard everything from you . . . if you guys cooperate."

"If we . . ." Gordon started, ". . . cooperate? Are you threatening us?"

"It doesn't matter," I said. "We're on vacation . . . I mean, we're not talking about monsters this week. So, that's that."

"Talking about monsters or not," she said, "I still need your help. I'd go there myself, but I can't find Raven Hill on any maps, and I've wandered around town day after day looking for the place."

"It has a way of keeping out unwanted visitors," I said.

"Wait!" Shane said. "How did you hear EVERYTHING? We might have gotten sloppy at the lunch table recently, but in the beginning, we kept things to a whisper—and we always speak in code."

"You were speaking in code?" she asked. "I didn't even know."

"It doesn't matter," Shane said. "What I want to know is how you actually HEARD everything. I've never seen you sitting near our table."

"You never saw me because I was born without a sense of smell," she said matter-of-factly.

We all looked at each other. Even Ben.

"I have an extremely sharp sense of hearing," she

added. “My poor nose gave all of its powers to my ears.”

“It looks like your eyes might have helped out as well,” snickered Gordon.

Nabila eyed Gordon through her thick lenses and continued, “Do you know how some people say they can hear a pin drop?”

“Yes,” we all said.

“Well,” she said, “I actually *can* hear a pin drop. I can hear the flight attendant’s shoes coming toward us, and I know that she has wet paper towels with her because I heard her turn the sink on, hold something in it, and squeeze out excess water.”

Sure enough, a concerned-looking flight attendant came down the aisle.

“Oh dear,” she said, looking at the mess.

We all forgot that Ben had barfed. We were hypnotized by Nabila’s tale. Even Ben forgot he had barfed—the flight attendant had to ask him the same question twice: “Didn’t you know there was a barf bag in the seat in front of you?”

“Nope,” he said simply, and grabbed the paper towels as the attendant passed them over.

“Sorry. This is his first time on a plane,” I explained.

There was a pause as Ben started to clean up.

“You need any more of this stuff?” he asked Nabila, holding up the dripping paper towels.

Behind us, Gordon gagged slightly.

"No," she said. "I've collected more than I possibly need to run my calculations."

The flight attendant looked at Nabila strangely as she grabbed the paper towels from Ben. But, before she could ask any questions, the intercom crackled and the captain announced that we'd be landing soon.

The flight attendant motioned to Gordon and Shane and said, "Please sit down."

"Yes, ma'am," Shane said politely as she walked away, and then turned to Nabila. "Wait! Why do you care about the monsters at the retirement home?"

"Ever since I was a little girl, I've been obsessed with American monster movies. Vampires. Werewolves. Mummies. I learned all about Halloween. Celebrating Halloween in America for the first time was amazing, but that was make-believe. What you guys are doing is *real,* and I can assist. I know things. I know a lot about mummification. I've read the ancient Egyptian *Book of the Dead*—"

"Interesting hobbies," said Shane, his eyebrow raised.

"—and I could help you guys in more ways than you can imagine."

With that, she sat down in her seat and looked forward.

My friends and I passed each other strange glances.

Wild Life

We arrived in Orlando in the early afternoon. While waiting in front of the terminal for a bus to take us to Cape Canaveral, I walked over to Mr. Stewart.

"Are we going right to Kennedy Space Center?" I asked him, trying my best to ignore Lunch Lady, who stood right next to him.

"That's the plan!" Mr. Stewart said with a smile. "We have orientation and then we will meet with an astronaut. Did you know there's always at least one astronaut answering questions there?"

"I did," I squealed, barely able to hold in my excitement.

Meanwhile, Coach Grey and all of the football players, Gordon included, were gathered at one side of the bus

stop. There seemed to be a lot of high-fiving and muscle flexing going on. I've never understood athletes, but Gordon looked happy. I guess he was right—we each had our own things and that was okay.

I walked from Mr. Stewart over to Shane and Ben, who were standing alone at the other side of the bus stop.

"Man this weather is supreme!" yelled Shane. "I could totally get used to this."

"I dunno," said Ben, "this humidity is a little nasty. I'm feeling pretty clammy."

"Aren't you always feeling clammy?" I asked.

"The weather is much, much hotter in Cairo," said Nabila, from out of nowhere.

"Ah!" I yelled and jumped.

The idea of meeting with an actual astronaut had made me forget about Nabila. But here she was, walking toward us with a bottle of water in her hand and a braces-filled grin on her face.

"Is it really?" Ben asked Nabila. "I don't know if I'd make it there."

"We'll see," she said with a wink, and handed Ben the bottled water. "Here, I thought you could use this."

"Aw, thanks," he said, and blushed for the fourth time that day. (I'd been counting.)

Two buses arrived, and everyone pushed and shoved their way on board. Ben and Nabila headed onto the first bus with Lunch Lady.

Shane reached out to stop them, but I pulled his arm back.

"Just let them go," I said, and walked toward the second bus.

I headed to the back of the bus, and dropped down in the very last row with a FLUMP.

"What's wrong?" asked Shane, slumping down in the seat next to me. "This is supposed the best day of your life, Space Boy."

"I feel like we'll never get a break from Raven Hill. First Lunch Lady shows up for the trip, and now all Nabila wants to talk about are the monsters. That's the last thing I want to discuss. We all agreed, no monsters on this trip."

"Ben knows to keep quiet, and he's the only one she wants to talk to," Shane said. "As for Lunch Lady, so what if Director Z sent her to keep an eye on us? We're not going to say *anything*. It was probably just her turn to chaperone, anyway."

"She's not just chaperoning," I said. "Something's going on, I know it."

"Stop worrying," said Shane. "Even if something *is* going on, there's nothing you can do about it. Just relax—we're heading to Kennedy Space Center, remember."

Forty minutes later, we arrived at Kennedy Space Center.

"See?" said Shane. "Nothing to worry about. We made it!"

I had seen a million pictures, I had spent hours on Google Maps zooming into the facilities, but I never thought it would look like this. There were very few buildings—it was mostly swamp. But that was okay—this swampy wonderland hid the mysteries of the universe. We passed by launchpads scorched by powerful rockets. We passed by crazy-looking radar equipment. *What star system is it observing?* I wondered—just one of a billion questions blasting through my brain.

I stared out of the window with my mouth wide open and moaned, "I. Can't. WAIT!"

When we passed the huge tower that used to house the space shuttles, even the jocks stared with bug eyes.

The buses pulled into the parking lot of the Visitor Complex.

Mr. Stewart rose out of seat and turned to face us. "Please exit the bus in an orderly fashion and form a line outside," he announced.

"It better be a *straight* line," grunted Coach Grey. "I don't want to see any sloppiness out there today."

Once off of the bus, Gordon, Ben, and Nabila walked toward us.

"So," said Gordon, "are you psyched or what? This

must be like Christmas morning for you!"

"Yeah, what are we going to do first?" asked Ben.

"Moon rock," I said without hesitation. "I have to touch me some moon rock!"

"Are any of the monsters you work with from space?" asked Nabila loudly.

Lunch Lady squinted her eyes in our direction.

She walked toward us to investigate, but something stopped her in her tracks!

The front of the first bus was parked up against a swampy gulley. Something was growling and snapping in the gully. Something monstrous!

"Aaaaaahhhhhh!" a few of the girls and more than one football player screamed and headed toward the Visitor Complex.

"No, wait!" yelled Mr. Stewart. "Everyone back on the bus, immediately!"

"You heard the man," barked Coach Grey. "Get your keisters back on these buses on the double! NOW!"

A second monstrous form appeared and began thrashing around with the first. A flock of cranes standing in the gully began to flutter their wings. Suddenly one vanished in an explosion of feathers and water. Then another. These monsters were hungry. And they were coming right at us.

"I wonder if cranes taste like chicken," said Shane as he leaned forward to get a better look.

Ignoring his question, I grabbed Shane's arm and ran back to the bus. "I *knew* it!" I yelled. "I knew that the Director would ruin it for us."

Kids crammed in front of the bus doors, desperate to get on. A panicked jock pushed a girl out of his way so hard that she fell and rolled toward the gully.

The water bubbled and a slick, leathery form rose out of the muck to meet her. Now we all leaned forward to get a better look.

"Get back!" yelled Coach Grey, and he lobbed a fastball at the monster's head.

With a splash and a growl, the monster was knocked back.

Coach scooped up the girl, who moaned, "It has teeeeeth! So many teeth!"

Once we were back on the bus, we had a better view of the vile creatures.

"I'm not sure if this was Director Z's work," said Shane, pointing out of the window. "Look!"

Two giant alligators emerged from the gully and crept up into the parking lot. They stopped in front of the buses, warming themselves in the late afternoon sun.

"Well," said Mr. Stewart, "it looks like we got a little Biology instead of Astronomy today. You're looking at two North American alligators, which are common to this area of Florida."

Mr. Stewart turned to the bus driver. "Mack, can you drive us directly to the entrance?"

"Wait!" a girl screamed. "There's another alligator behind the bus!"

"We're surrounded," said Shane, pointing out of the window. "There must be a dozen of them out there."

Forty-five minutes later we were still seated in the sweltering hot bus, watching as the alligators slowly made their way back into the swamp.

"I'm losing my mind," I said to Shane. "We're so close to Kennedy Space Center—and all we can do is stare at it."

"On the bright side," added Shane, "at least no one asked us to clean up after the gators . . . or serve them lunch. That's a step in right direction."

Finally, the buses left the parking lot, drove past the Visitor Complex, and . . . headed back onto the main road.

"Wait," I said, jumping from my seat. "What?"

"Ladies and gentlemen," Mr. Stewart said, "considering the time, we've decided to go directly to our lodging and unpack."

"Noooooooo!" I screamed.

"Chris." Mr. Stewart looked at me strangely. "My decision is final. Don't worry—we'll have plenty of time to explore the facility tomorrow."

I looked at Kennedy Space Center, and had a sinking feeling that I'd never make it back.

Fart Machines

Kennedy Space Center had long faded from view by the time the buses pulled into our "lodgings."

"Way to go, Rio Vista Middle School," Shane said as he saw where we were staying . . . Zed's CraZy DiZcount CabinZ. "Couldn't you find anyplace crummier for us to stay?"

"What were you expecting?" I replied. "A five-star hotel?" I didn't care where we stayed, I just wanted to drop off my bags and head back to the space center.

"I take back what I said," Shane said, patting me on the back as we stepped off the bus. "Look, the beach is just down that path. Thank you, Rio Vista!"

In the parking lot, Ben and Gordon were waiting

for us. And, of course, Nabila stood close by Ben's side. It was a good thing she couldn't smell Ben, who still reeked of warm barf.

"I have to get to my cabin," said Nabila. "I want to freshen up before we meet Mr. Stewart on the beach for the welcome announcement. I'll see you boys later."

"Yeah, much later," grumbled Gordon. "You've got A LOT of freshening up to do."

"Whew," I said as she walked away.

"Wow, she's special, guys," said Ben. "I mean, really smart! And an expert on Egyptology. I think we should introduce her to the mummies."

"Yeah, we know what you think, lover boy!" Gordon said. "But I don't want her cramping our style."

"Me neither," I said. "We can tell her how to get to Raven Hill when we get back from the trip. Director Z will be happy we found fresh blood."

After we all tried our best to "freshen up" in our CraZy Cabin, we went down to the beach. It was cool and breezy, with waves gently lapping up against the shore.

"Man," Shane said with a sigh, "I could really get used to this. Nice."

"Yeah," I said. "It's so quiet and—"

"Hey, guys!" we heard a shout from farther down the beach.

Nabila was walking over.

"Arrrgh!" I harrumphed. "When is she going to get that we just don't want to hang out?"

"Hi, Ben," she said as she approached us. "How are you feeling?"

"Pretty good, actually," Ben said, and he got a little red in the face.

Ben was not blushing for the fifth time—he was already starting to get a sunburn.

"That's a nice fanny pack you have," he said nervously.

"Oh, thank you," she replied. "I always have it on me. I even sleep with it. I never know when I might need something!"

Mr. Stewart and the chaperones made their way up the beach.

"So," Ben shyly continued with Nabila. "What—"

"Shhhh . . ." Nabila said, and then whipped out a small notebook and pen from her fanny pack. "I think they're going to give us the outline of the week's events."

Mr. Stewart said, "Welcome to Cape Canaveral! We planned a lot of fun events for everyone, but due to today's unfortunate incident with the overgrown reptiles of Kennedy Space Center, we're going to scale back a bit. I've decided that there will be no snorkeling in the nearby springs. Nor will there be any swimming. We're just going to stick to Kennedy Space Center—"

"Yeah!" I yelled. I knew that Shane was depressed by the news, but we came for the space center, not the beach.

Mr. Stewart continued: "—with a little bit of bird-watching at Cape Canaveral National Seashore."

A whole bunch of *Aw, mans* and *Nos* floated up from the crowd of kids.

He went on to talk about all of the rules and regulations and blah-blah-blah boring stuff. He ended with an announcement that we'd all have a BBQ dinner that night on the beach, cooked up, of course, by Lunch Lady.

"I'm sorry, Shane," I said, and put my hand on his shoulder. "You should wear your surfing sharks to Kennedy Space Center. Want to just sit down and enjoy the view?"

"I was really excited to go snorkeling," said Nabila. "I brought along an invention I've been working on that I hoped to test out."

"What's that?" Shane asked.

"It's a device that attracts fish," she said, and pulled a small, black rectangular device out of her fanny pack. "Someone's already created an iPhone app, but I really wanted mine to be waterproof. Since, as you know, most fish are underwater."

"How does it work?" Ben asked.

"Well," she said, "it uses natural sounds to attract fish—small fish sucking on rocks, shrimp shells rubbing together, herring flatulence . . ."

"Wait," Shane said. "Do you mean herring *farts*?"

"Yes," said Nabila. "Herring communicate by farting, and the theory is that hearing their farts could attract other fish—fish that like herring. At the least, it should attract other farting herring. I was interested to see if more fish approached me than approached others while we were snorkeling."

"Oh, man, that's hilarious!" Gordon laughed. "I wonder if Lunch Lady is going to barbecue some farting herring tonight?"

Shane, Gordon, and I cracked up.

"I think it's cool," said Ben. He gave Nabila an approving nod.

Gordon continued chuckling uncontrollably. "Wait, wait! I've got something like your device on my iPhone. Check this out."

He whipped out his iPhone and, after touching the screen a few times there was a noisy, wet, sloppy FLLLLUUUURRRRT!

He laughed and touched his screen one more time. This one was higher pitched.

FEEEEEPT!

And another.

FWWWAAAAAAAAAP!

"Wait, wait," he said, practically crying now, "let me add one more."

There was a PING as he touched the screen, followed by a countdown.

"THREE!"

Gordon moved the phone down to his posterior.

"TWO!"

He stopped laughing for a moment and concentrated.

"ONE!"

He farted a long, juicy fart. He started to chuckle near the end and it came out with a little *fit-fit-fit* sound.

I couldn't help laughing. Shane and Ben joined in.

"Oh, man," said Shane. "It almost sounded like he was saying something. Ha-ha-ha!"

Nabila gave Gordon the stink-eye and said, "Oh, no, that's nothing like my device. My device attracts fish. Yours attracts idiots."

She stormed away as we laughed our heads off, and I looked forward to a fish dinner with my friends.

Something's Fishy

After our beach BBQ, Shane, Ben, Gordon, and I all headed back up to our stuffy old cabin. I was too excited to sleep. And even if I wanted to, it would be impossible to block out the sound of Gordon snoring away on the top bunk across from me. Shane, however, was fast asleep, lying stiff as a board on his back, but with a look of content on his face. He even slept like a karate master.

Ben must have heard me shuffling above him in my bunk. "Are you awake, too?" he asked.

"Yeah," I whispered back.

"Is it me, or was the fish extra fishy tonight?" Ben asked. "It kind of tasted like that last batch of Mac 'n' Sneeze."

"Fish is supposed to be fishy," I said. "Or it wouldn't be fish. Would you want chicken to taste like cow?"

"Well, at least I got to eat dinner on the beach with Nabila," he said, and sighed.

I saw where this was going.

"She's OFF LIMITS, dude!" I hissed.

"Hey," Ben said, "she's just a special kind of girl."

"That's true," I said. "I thought Gordon's fart library would keep her away, but even after that, she sat down with us at dinner."

"Sat down with *me*," said Ben. "Even on the plane. Most girls usually run screaming when I barf. But this girl is . . . different."

I didn't know what to say next, but I knew for sure that if Ben fell for Nabila that we'd be forced to let her into our circle, and I'd lose a friend to puppy love. So, I changed the subject.

"Can you believe that fish talk by farting?" I asked. "No wonder Gil likes to fart so much. He's just saying, 'Hello!'"

Ben started to giggle.

"The way he goes at it," Ben said, "he's saying a WHOLE lot more than 'Hello!' He's reciting the Declaration of Independence!"

"Parlez vous fartzes?" I chortled.

"Habla fartspañol?" Ben countered.

We laughed until we cried, and then as we caught

our breath, we smelled something funny.

"Whew," I said, "speaking of nasty smells."

"Ugh," said Ben. "What is that?"

The smell was superfunky and overpowering. I put my T-shirt over my nose and mouth. Ben did the same.

"Where the heck is that coming from?" Ben asked.

I climbed down from my bunk and sniffed around.

"It smells fine outside," I said as I looked out the window.

"Good; I'm coming over there," said Ben.

With a snort, Gordon sat up on the bunk bed.

"Dudes, put your shoes back on," he moaned, still half asleep. "That's some serious athlete's foot I'm smellin'."

It smelled like something from the ocean had flopped into our room and died—worse than the swamp creature—but I couldn't see anything in the room.

I kept sniffing around. I sniffed Shane's feet. I sniffed the closet. I got down and sniffed the floorboards.

"Ach!" I almost choked. "It's coming from under us."

"Great," said Ben. "What the heck crawled into the crawl space and died?"

I sniffed one more time, and the smell was even worse.

That's when there was a BANG, and our cabin shook.

"What the . . . ?" Gordon swayed on his bunk.

BANG!

This time one of the floorboards cracked, just in front of Shane and Gordon's bunk.

BANGCRACKBANG!

The bunk beds swayed. Under the floorboards, a low, wet hiss could be heard.

There was a pause and then . . .

CRAAAACK!

A huge, wet worm with hundreds of slimy, squirmy legs burst through the floor and slithered out between the broken wood.

HISSSSSS!

As more of the worm slithered into the room, the stench went from overpowering to painfully eye-watering.

"Aahhh!" Shane yelled. He was finally awake. He leaped up and landed on the floor in a karate pose.

The worm towered over Shane, writhing and wet, and opened its huge, slimy hole of a mouth.

SCHLUUUUUUUCK!

It paused for a minute, and then swung over to Gordon.

"Aaaaarrggh!" Gordon yelled, and then he squeezed himself between the wall and the bunk bed, pushing it toward the massive sea worm.

The bed knocked the worm over, right onto me!

"Oof!" I grunted . . .

. . . and collapsed on the floor. The worm's limp head crashed down in my lap.

It was stunned, but just for a moment. It turned its eyeless head toward me and opened a mucus-filled mouth.

HIIIISSSSSS!

The smell overwhelmed my senses. I was stunned. But not because it was terrible. Because it smelled so good.

"Chris!" Shane screamed. "To your left!"

I looked up to see my bunk bed coming down and rolled out of the way just in time.

SPLUNK!

With a juicy crack, the bed landed on the head of the worm-beast, and it twitched under the weight.

"Let's get out of here!" Ben yelled, and we ran for the door.

But before we could get outside, two more worms burst through the door.

We scrambled to the window.

And two more worms were waiting for us!

They shot out in a flash. The two at the door reared up in front of Gordon and Shane, opened their mouth-holes wide, and then . . .

GULP!

. . . came down on my friends so fast that I didn't even see them get swallowed.

"Nooooooo!" I screamed, and rushed at the worms, which had already turned to slither back out the door.

"Chris!" I could hear a muffled voice. "Chriiiiiiis!"

I couldn't tell if it was Shane. Or Gordon. Or both.

Before I could reach either worm, my feet were brought out from under me. I went flying forward, and bumped my head hard. I saw stars, and was too weak to fight as the worm grabbed me with its sticky mouth and started to slurp up my legs, my face dragging along the floor. I could feel its muscles ripple all around me as I was pulled in deeper and deeper.

I was able to turn just in time to see Ben, terrified, also being swallowed. He clutched two phones in his hands.

"Catch," he gasped, and tossed me mine.

I grabbed it, and wondered, why, as a soon-to-be-dead man, I wanted this. Perhaps Ben wanted to make sure we connected in the afterlife?

It didn't matter. Nothing mattered. We were worm meat. Still . . . I clutched the phone as the worm slurped me up into its hot guts.

Good-Smellin' Guts

It smelled amazing inside the worm. A. May. ZING. It smelled exactly like the roasted nuts you might find at a carnival or fair, but even sweeter. Like the roasted-nut guys were cooking the nuts in a vat of cotton candy juice.

I felt warm. I felt happy. I felt . . . safe.

I curled up into the warm guts and thought about taking a nap. I was almost off to dreamland—

When my phone rang in my hand.

The light from the screen illuminated the guts and I was once again reminded that I was not at some local fair, but inside a massive sea worm. I was wrapped in the stomach of the creature, covered in goop and black stuff. Veins pumped thick, black blood just through the surface of the stomach skin.

Suddenly I didn't feel so safe.

I accepted the call and slowly, slimily pulled the phone up to my ear. It was difficult, and it felt like the creature's stomach muscles were trying to slow me down along the way.

Finally, I got the phone up to my ear.

"Hello?" I asked

"Hi, Chrissy!" a voice squealed with excitement on the other end of the line.

"Hi, Mom," I said as unexcitedly as I could.

"Well, sheesh!" she bubbled. "Thanks for picking up. You usually just call me back later."

I had no idea what to say to my mother, but I had to get her off the phone.

"Well," I stumbled. "We made it here just fine today, and the wildlife is really . . . wild! In fact I have to run up the nature trail real quick—someone saw a . . . um . . . hippo."

The guts were making me delirious.

"Hippo?" My mother sounded confused. "Chrissy, it doesn't even sound like you're outside—you sound like you're inside."

If you only knew, I thought.

"Okay, Ma!" I yelled. "I gotta go. Love you!"

I hung up the phone and was once again plunged

into the sweet, sweet darkness of the sea worm. I really wanted to nap, but before laying my head on the squishy stomach lining, I made a very important call.

"Huh . . . hullo?" Ben purred on the other end.

I had clearly woken him up.

"Hey!" I yelled. "It's me, Chris! We're still alive!"

"This is so weird," Ben said. "What's happening? Does your worm smell like the best brand of dryer sheets ever? Like, mixed with really, really good dishwashing detergent and body wash?"

"Well, my worm smells really good, but like the best carnival sweets you could ever imagine."

"Weird! It made me so happy in here that I just . . ."

". . . fell asleep," I finished. "Yeah, I would have too, if my mother hadn't just called me. This is really, really weird."

"It doesn't look like we're being digested," said Ben. "I'm not being burned by any acid. You?"

"Nope," I said, looking at my pale-white-as-usual arm in the glow of the phone.

"Listen," Ben said.

When we were first scooped up by the sea worms, we could hear hundreds of legs stomping along the ground, and the guts were much more jiggly.

Now all we could hear was a soft *swishhhhhh.*

"We're in the water," I said. "Oh, man, where are they taking us?"

"Do Shane or Gordon have their cell phones?" Ben asked.

"I have no idea," I said. "I'll call them and see if they answer."

"Okay," said Ben. "Enjoy your good-smellin' worm. If they'd smelled as bad on the inside as they do on the outside, I would have died in two minutes."

Ben hung up.

I tried calling Shane but before I could get halfway through his number on the third try, my fingers slipped off of the keypad and I fell into a deep, relaxed sleep.

I woke up FAST.

The muscles of the sea worm rippled around me. They pushed and squeezed—I could barely breathe. Then a light appeared above me, and I heard a retching sound.

Below, a black ooze bubbled up around my feet, and the sweet smell of roasted nuts and cotton candy was immediately erased. It once again smelled like centuries-old rotten fish.

WHHHURP!

WHHHHHARRRFFF!

The worm retched and coughed, and I slowly,

painfully made my way up toward the light, the muscles squeezing me tightly the whole way.

The smell was absolutely horrific, and I didn't know how much more I could take. The worm was trying to get me out, but it was just too slow.

The black goo had made its way up to my waist, and I was about to pass out. I had to speed things up somehow.

My arms were pinned to my side. My legs were pushed straight down.

I only had one weapon . . . my mouth.

I opened up as wide as I could, coughing and spitting, and

CHOMP!

I bit the tender stomach lining of the sea worm.

I could hear an angry hiss, and the sea worm's body rippled. It squeezed me with its guts even harder.

"Arrrrggghhhh!" I yelled.

The pain was intense.

And then, suddenly,

SPLOOT!

I shot out of the worm, and into the blinding light.

I was completely dazed and confused, but I knew two things right away.

I was rolling through the most beautiful beach I had ever seen in my life and . . .

I stopped right in front of the feet of Director Z!

Beach Bums

"YOU were the one who sent the worms!" I coughed through a mouthful of sand and sea worm gunk.

"Indeed," said Director Z.

"I knew you would do something like this," I said.

Director Z and two Nurses stood on a white sand beach, surrounded by sunbathing monsters—some in creaky wooden chairs, some on ragged, thin towels. It was bright—and HOT. It felt a hundred times hotter than it had felt on Cape Canaveral. Beyond the beach was a thick jungle, and from out of the jungle, tall, white resort towers pushed into the sky.

Behind me, I could hear the giant sea worm splash back into the water. It burped one last painful burp and disappeared under the waves.

I couldn't believe it. I closed my eyes and shook my head, but when I opened my eyes again, I still saw old monsters up and down the beautiful beach. I tried to stand, but stumbled backward and rolled toward the surf. The Nurses came down to help me.

"Hold me up to his face," I ordered one Nurse.

He gave me a strange look, but did as he was told. I was nose to nose with Director Z, covered in sandy black gunk. I shook with anger in the hands of the Nurse.

"What are you doing!?" I screamed. "You ruined my Dream Trip, just like I knew you would!!!"

"Chris, you might not feel the same, but it's wonderful to see you," said Director Z calmly. "I do *very* much apologize for the mode of transportation I selected to get you to Paradise Island."

"Paradise Island . . . in the Bermuda Triangle?" I asked. "That's where Herr Direktor Detlef's retirement home is . . ."

"That is correct," said Director Z. "The important news Herr Direktor Detlef was never able to announce—he'd be swapping facilities with us—as a congratulations for defeating the sussuroblats. We left that very same night, but you left before I could tell you. He and his residents are now at Raven Hill."

"Great for you guys, but why are *we* here?" I demanded, still staring Director Z directly in the eyes.

"And why did you send worms to get us?"

"First off," Director Z said, "I'd like to point out that it could have been worse—the witches put several spells on the sea worms, which led to a much more pleasant journey. The stomachs of the beasts were charmed with a smellgood spell and a hibernation spell. You fell asleep comfortably, I assume?"

"Yeah, I guess I took a little nap," I growled.

"You had more than a nap," said Director Z. "It's at least a six-hour journey by sea worm to this island from Cape Canaveral, and I'm sure for you it felt like . . ."

"Fifteen minutes!" I said, flabbergasted. "Why didn't you just ask us to come with you?" I asked. "It would have been a better trip than the one I just took."

"We didn't need you until now. Plus, I knew that you were fed up with Raven Hill, and quite frankly, I think you had every right to be. I've been working you hard, and despite all your efforts, the residents have been quite rude. So I let you go on your field trip, but had Ms. Veracruz keep a close eye on you in case you were needed."

"What about the fact that four students are now missing?" I asked.

"Ms. Veracruz slipped a short-term-memory-erasing serum into the breakfast of everyone in your group so that they will forget that you were even with them. Everything has been taken care of, and I'm grateful that you're here. You see, we have a major problem, Chris, and I need your help."

I was still angry I was missing out on Kennedy Space Center, but what could I do? The main reason we wanted a break from Raven Hill was because the monsters really didn't need us. Now that I knew they needed us, I felt ready to help.

"Put me down," I said to the Nurse.

The Nurse put me down and Director Z crouched down closer to my face, speaking softly. "Several of the residents have suffered a severe lebensplasm loss," he explained, "but we can't tell *how* they are being drained. They seem perfectly happy one moment, and then the very next, they're agitated and annoyed, lashing out and biting—harming others and themselves. It's like they've been given a strange strength at the same time that they've been drained."

"But how can we help?" I asked. "And where are my friends?"

"I made sure your sea worm arrived first," Director Z said, "so that we could talk. I figured you might have a few questions. The others should be along shortly. As we're not sure what we're defending ourselves against, I'm not yet exactly sure how you gentlemen *can* help. However, you helped defend Raven Hill from the sussuroblats, so I'm sure you can help us here with whatever enemy we face. And, I can assure you, I will *more* than make up for your missed trip to Kennedy Space Center."

His normally cool face became sad and tired. He headed into the crowd of sunbathing monsters.

"Please join me," he said.

We weaved our way through the old monsters. The swamp creature was applying sun cream to his scaly body. A group of witches stood up and ran toward the water, cackling in their long black bathing gowns. All of the banshees lay facedown on threadbare towels, enjoying a bit of sun on their backs.

We walked a few feet past the last sunbathers.

"Now, I don't want to alarm my staff or my residents," said Director Z, "which is why I'm trying to be as discreet as possible, but this is an extremely worrisome situation. We've absolutely never seen anything like this before. One of the mummies unwrapped himself and walked right into the ocean. A witch went mad and hexed a few of the zombies—luckily she was so deranged, the effects were minimal. Flowers grew out of their ears.

"As you can see, not many of them have been affected—most are actually amazingly healthy and relaxed after only a few days here. You'll see that everyone is much better behaved. But, the ones who have been drained . . ."

Director Z stared at the crashing blue waves for a moment, his face growing even sadder.

"Yes?" I asked.

"Well, Chris, they are mere shells of their former selves. In my history as Director, I've never seen any residents drained so fast. I think we may lose the residents in mass numbers unless we can figure out what's going on here."

"Okay, okay!" I said, now just as worried as Director Z. "I'm ready to solve your mystery."

The dark frown left Director Z's face, and he straightened his suit.

"And, while you solve the mystery, you should also enjoy all the perks of a private tropical island. As soon as your friends arrive, I'll give you a tour of the facility. I'm sure you'll want to see where all the Jacuzzis are, and knowing the layout of the facility will also be helpful in piecing clues together."

We walked back toward the sunbathers.

Vacations Make Me Sick

Director Z and I walked past a group of sunbathing old vampires on the beach, their wrinkled bodies on display. They wore a stomach-churning choice of swimwear: Speedos. Their hairy chests smoldered slightly in the morning sunlight.

"Chris!" said Grigore, one of the vampires. "It is vonderful to see you here!"

He got up to say hello, grinning a sharp-toothed grin from ear to ear. He had helped us defeat the sussuroblats, but like the other monsters, Grigore was usually grumpy and hard to deal with. I was surprised to see him so happy.

"What are you doing in the sun?" I asked.

"One of the few benefits of being a weak old vampire," he said, "is that the sun affects me very little."

"But the smoke . . ." I said, smelling bacon in the air.

"Smoke?" Grigore looked confused. "I'm smoking? Sheesh. I just applied an SPF 5,000 a few minutes ago."

"Yes, you gentlemen might want to find a palm tree," said Director Z. "You don't want to overdo it. That being said, I think you're getting quite a nice tan, old man."

Before I could ask Director Z any more questions, there was a huge splash, and three sea worms crawled out of the crashing waves. They reared up, retched loudly, and spit out my three friends, before returning to the water.

"Ah," said Director Z, "right on time!"

Director Z called a few Nurses down to help my friends, who began to stir on the sand.

Ben and Shane grunted as the Nurses helped them to their feet. Gordon appeared to be asleep. His head bobbed on his chest.

I walked down with the Director to talk with them.

"Dude," said Shane, "why are we here?"

"The monster juice supply is in danger," I said. "Director Z ordered the worms to bring us here. We have to help."

"And why are *they* here?" asked Ben, rubbing his eyes in disbelief.

"They've traded facilities with Herr Direktor

Detlef's residents," I replied. "Welcome to Paradise Island!"

"Ohhhhhh," Ben and Shane said.

Gordon's head came up so quick I swear I heard his neck crack.

"Wow!" said Gordon, screaming through clenched teeth. "This place is beautiful! Is this the Cape Canaveral Alligator Refuge Thingamajiggy? How did we get here? Why do I smell like my mother's roast chicken?"

Gordon drooled a little bit and then passed out again. The Nurse held on tight.

"Shane, what did your worm smell like?" I asked.

"Oh yeah!" he said. "It was the strangest thing. It smelled like the inside of a jack-o'-lantern when you burn a candle in it—specifically, the lid of the jack-o'-lantern, when you pull it off and give it a whiff at the end of the night. I think that's my favorite smell of all time, actually."

"But of course," said the Director. "The smellgood spell the witches cast on the innards of the sea worms give them the odor of your favorite smell."

"Cleaning products," said Ben.

"Carnival food," I said.

Gordon's head slowly came up once again.

"Gordon, is the smell of your mother's roast chicken your favorite smell?" I asked.

"No, I hate my mother's roast chicken," Gordon

growled, staring into the distance like a zombie. "Where is the rest of my team? We have practice with Coach Grey tonight. Coach. Practice. We. Have. Roast . . . chicken?"

He looked at his hands and began to cry.

"Gordon?" Ben asked, "Are you okay?"

He looked at Ben and screamed. He shook and spat in the Nurse's arms, gurgling and frothing at the mouth. A few of the old monsters turned toward the noise.

"Gordon!" I yelled.

"Nurse Gigg, release him at once," Director Z commanded. "He's seizing so hard he'll break his bones if you hold on to him!"

Nurse Gigg dropped Gordon, who hit the sand and flopped around like a piranha on a carpet. He kicked sand onto a few of the sunbathing mummies, who looked up in surprise.

Shane bent down to help Gordon, but Director Z pushed him back.

"There's nothing we can do now," said Director Z. "It's up to him to fight it."

"Fight what?" Ben asked.

"He's having an allergic reaction to the sea worm," Director Z said.

"Gwaaaaah!" Gordon yelled.

He arched his back until I thought it would break, and then lay terribly still.

"Gordon?"

Trouble in Paradise

Director Z kneeled down next to Gordon, and checked his pulse. He then stared off in the distance for a long time. Almost all of the monsters got up and shuffled down to the water's edge to investigate.

"Well?" asked Frederick, the old stitched-together monster. "Is he dead?"

Ben, Shane, and I stared in shock, waiting for Director Z's answer.

"His pulse is slow," he finally said, "but it's there. We must get him to the infirmary at once."

He waved Nurse Gigg back over.

"Quickly," he commanded.

Nurse Gigg bent over, picked Gordon up, and threw

him over his shoulder in one smooth motion.

"Is he going to be okay?" asked Ben.

"Yes," said Director Z. "But we must act swiftly."

Director Z and the Nurse ran up the beach and into the jungle.

Ben, Shane, and I stood on the beach, dumbfounded. Shane finally broke the silence.

"Well, what are we waiting for?" he said, and sprinted up to the path, which was marked with a tiki torch.

Ben and I followed.

"Wow," Ben said as we ran deep into the jungle. "It's cold in here. Where did the sun go? I can't even see the buildings anymore."

"Look—Director Z is just up there," I said.

We ran up to meet him. Nurse Gigg was a few yards ahead. Gordon's head bobbed up and down as he plowed forward.

We caught up to Nurse Gigg, and kept running. Strange noises escaped from the jungle, but none was stranger than the low, deep growls that shook the leaves.

"RIIIIIBBBBBBIIIIT."

"What the heck was that?" gasped Ben. "It sounds like a massive frog!"

"Perhaps we should move a little faster, gentlemen," said Director Z. The Nurse repositioned Gordon on his shoulder and we picked up our pace.

"RIIIIIBBBBBIIIITTTBRAINS!"

"Brains?!" I said. "Did that frog just ribbit, 'brains'?"

"RIBBBRRAAAIINNNS!"

"RIBBBBRRRAAAIINNS!"

"RIBBBBBRRRAAAIIINNNNNSSS!"

"Make that four or five frogs," Director Z said.

The vegetation ahead of us shook, and a massive frog, slick with slime and covered in sores and gashes, flopped out of the jungle.

"BRAAAAAIIIINNNNNS," it croaked, and flopped toward us.

Two more frogs flopped out of the jungle just in front of the Nurse. They shot their bloody tongues out of their mouths, nearly tripping him. He jumped to the side, kicking one in the head with a wet SQUISH and we ran past them.

"Almost there," Director Z said.

FLOP. FLOP. FLOP. FLOP.

"There are a bunch of them behind us!" screamed Ben.

I took a peek behind my shoulder. The frogs were bright red and green, like the poisonous frogs I've see on the Internet. But these were huge! They stumbled over each other on the narrow path, tongues lashing.

"Here we are," said Director Z.

We approached two Nurses, who stood guard on either side of the path.

"Four, perhaps five zombie frogs are right behind us," he yelled at the Nurses as we passed. "Please halt them, and arrange a frog-leg fricassee for dinner."

We spilled out of the jungle into the resort. It looked like the kind of place parents would go for a romantic getaway. All the walkways were open to a blue sky. As we passed a small open-air theater, I could see Horace, the old organ player, playing steel drums for a small audience of old monsters. We flew past an infinity pool. A zombie floated facedown in a bubbly Jacuzzi.

"The Jacuzzi better be heavily chlorinated," gasped Shane, "or I'll be sticking to the beach."

We ran farther back into the resort. The cool white adobe walls gave away once again to jungle, although this time we were in a clearing, and surrounded by the resort on all sides. There was a large hut set up in the center of the clearing, and out of the large hut came screaming and moaning.

"Oh dear," said Director Z. "I do hope the Nurses have everything under control."

We headed inside the thatch hut to find Nurses and witches frantically running around from bed to bed, doing their best to soothe demented old monsters.

"Griselda!" the Director called to one of the witches. "Please help me with this child immediately. He's had a severe reaction to your sea worm."

The Nurse threw Gordon onto an exam table, and

Griselda rushed over, opened up one of Gordon's eyes and peered inside. She then leaned down to listen to his breathing. We held our breaths.

"Hmmm," Griselda mumbled aloud to herself, "let's see . . . antihistamine spells . . ."

She held her hands high and chanted a spell.

Gordon sat up, gulped a lungful of air, and fell back in the bed.

Griselda turned to us and said, "He's going to be fine."

We stopped holding our breaths.

Gordon might have been on the road to recovery, but the others in the infirmary were not. The Director and the witch tended to Gordon while the three of us watched the panic.

"I didn't think there was any way these guys could look older," said Shane. "But, look at them—they're practically skin and bones."

"Yeah, but they're wild," said Ben. "Look at them kick around. They look old, but they act . . . possessed."

"I don't have a good feeling about this," I said.

We walked closer to Gordon's bed to have a better look. Director Z and Griselda were in a heated argument.

"Well, Zachary," said Griselda angrily, "I could probably do a better job if we had taken the time to pack the right herbs before leaving. These facilities are a mess! I'm a modern witch working with old materials here!"

"First off," said Director Z, "it's 'Boss' or 'Director.'

Secondly, I apologize for the facilities, but I'm told the witch doctor actually does a good job with the resources he has on the island. You may just need to tweak your recipes."

"Tweak the recipes?" she asked, flabbergasted. "Tweak the recipes, Zachary, dear? That's all I've been doing all day. And all I've gotten for it is a bunch of farting, angry old monsters."

Gordon stirred on the table. He moaned, but the two arguing adults didn't seem to notice him.

"Coach," he groaned. "Coach . . . am I up?"

"Um . . . Director Z." I pulled gently at his suit.

"What?!" he snapped at me.

I pointed at Gordon. Griselda continued her examination.

"Oh, yes, quite right," he mumbled. "Did you say 'farting old monsters'? Is the core issue digestive, Griselda?"

"Hmmm . . . ," Griselda said, staring at Gordon. "I believe all this one needs now is an herb-based restorative talisman."

She rummaged around every basket nearby, before grabbing a small doll made of leaves.

"Sage," she said, and held it out to Gordon. "Here, take it."

"Noooo," he whined. "I don't want that. Where's Coach?"

He looked around confused, searching for Coach Grey.

"Zachary," Griselda said one more time, and Director Z scowled. "I need to make sure this child, of his own free will, accepts my talisman before I cast a final spell. This could take a while. Why don't you touch base with the Nurses about the farting? They'll fill you in."

Before heading into the back of the hut and all of the screaming, frothing monsters, Shane gave Griselda a tip: "Put the herbs in a football, and pass it to him. He'll hold on to it tight then."

Ben snickered and we walked away.

There were three old monsters strapped to small, squeaking beds in the back of the hut. Each of them was fighting, gnashing his teeth and screaming.

"Let us go, and ve'll spare your life, beefcake," a vampire spat at his Nurse. He was practically rotting away in front of us.

"You look stringy and far too chewy," said an ancient-looking werewolf, "but we will tear you limb from limb and chew you down to your bones if you don't let us go. We need more juice—these are nearly dry!"

The werewolf howled so loud that his eyes bugged out. They popped, but didn't squirt—the juice stayed on him as if he were covered with a thin film, like saran wrap.

"What's wrong, guys?" asked Shane.

"Shut up, young one," said the dried-up zombie writhing on his bed. "You are neither ripe with the juice nor a tool worthy of manipulation. You are worthless to us. WORTHLESS."

"Nurses," said the director. "Please give me a status report."

"Boss," said a Nurse, "reason for lebensplasm drainage unknown. Residents appear to be covered by something. No herbs can help. Strange side effects."

"That's the most I've ever heard a Nurse talk," said Shane.

"This must be serious," I said. "The Nurses are talking. Director Z is freaking out. What's going on here?"

"What do you mean, strange side effects?" Director Z asked the Nurse. "Are these the digestive issues that Griselda had mentioned?"

"Not caused by drainage," said another Nurse. "Caused by herbs."

"Show me," said the Director.

The Nurse closest to him gulped and grabbed a sack of herbs from the floor. He jumped up on the bed and pinned the already strapped-in zombie with his knees. The zombie's head thrashed about and even more foam poured from his mouth.

"Look at that," said Ben. "The drool isn't dripping off his face; it's just pooled under his chin."

"It is quite bizarre," said the Director. "It would appear that he's captured by some invisible force that has sealed itself to his body. We can't even take a fluid sample to see how low his lebensplasm supply is."

"EEEEEEEEEEEEEE," the zombie screamed, and the other sick old monsters joined in, thrashing even harder. Dust rose from the dirt floor.

The Nurse took a large wad of freshly-ground herbs and shoved them directly into the zombie's screaming mouth.

"EEEEEEEEEE-gug."

The zombie swallowed, and for a minute, seemed to be calm. The other two monsters, on the other hand, went insane.

"Noooooo," they screamed, in unison, "he is ours now. We shall take him back."

The zombie's eyes blinked. He looked at the Director.

"So weak," he whispered. "Help me."

The zombie's eyes then went wide, and he grunted hard.

"Nooooo!" he wailed. "Not again!!!"

He grunted and spasmed, as if being attacked by some invisible force. He shuddered in his bed so hard that the Nurse was thrown off and onto the floor with an *"OOF."*

The zombie paused for a moment, gasped, and then . . .

BLLLLLLLUUUUURRRRRRFFFFFFT!

Let out the most earth-quaking, neighbor-waking fart I had ever heard in my life.

His body went limp for a few moments, and the other monsters were silent.

The Nurse on the floor got up slowly, and said, "Strongest herbal remedy . . . doesn't work."

He leaned down to check on the zombie, when suddenly . . .

RIIIIIIIIP!

The zombie's torso tore free from his arms, and he sprung forward, biting the neck of the Nurse. There was a meaty crunch as the zombie dug in deep and chewed frantically on the Nurse-flesh. The Nurse fell back with a grunt, and brought the zombie with him. The zombie's feet popped off the ends of his restraints.

"I'm free," he gurgled, and then used the stubs that were left at the bottom of his legs to run out of the hut.

The Nurse stood up, staggered, and fell back on the bed, which still had the wiggling limbs of the zombie shaking it. The other two monsters laughed and laughed.

"Is he okay?" shrieked Ben.

"Griselda! GRISELDA!!!"

Security Measures

“Should have moved,” the Nurse moaned. “Was too slow.”

He coughed up a wad of blood and passed out.

The other Nurses and witches immediately surrounded him and went to work.

“Wait,” said Ben. “Isn’t he going to be a zombie now?”

“Not likely,” said the Director. “The Nurses have undergone years of medical processing to assure that they are immune to vampirism, zombieism, werewolfism, mummification, and more.”

“Ooooh . . . ,” we all said. Finally, an explanation for why the Nurses never turned into monsters.

"He's going to make it," said Griselda. "That old zombie just missed the jugular."

One Nurse pulled out a huge needle and twine.

"But after these stitches," continued Griselda, "he's gonna have one heck of a scar."

"On the bright side, at least one of the Nurses will finally look different from the others," said Shane.

Someone screamed in the resort.

"That sounded like one of the banshees," said Director Z.

A Nurse came running through the door. "He's run into the jungle."

"We must institute security measures and capture that rogue zombie," said Director Z. "But I don't want the residents who have yet to be exposed to this dreadful sickness to know anything about it. They should be able to go about their daily lives—the better their moods, the stronger their lebensplasm will stay."

"I have an idea," I said. "Let's get them all into the theater for Ben's trivia. They love that stuff."

"Yeah," said Ben, "I could keep them distracted while you guys search for the zombie.

"They would all be safe in one place," said Director Z.

"Excellent!" I said. "So, I'll start the search for the rogue zombie with Shane . . ."

"WAIT," said a voice.

We all turned to see Gordon sitting up on his table.

"I'll go with you," said Gordon. "I'm a little amped up from my nap. Nap . . . wait, I was sleeping?"

"Gordon," said Ben. "Are you okay?"

"I feel GREAT," he said.

"Are you ready for your home game?" asked Shane.

"What!?" said Gordon. "I thought we were battling a rogue zombie."

"Welcome back, Gordon," said Director Z. "You and Chris should grab a half-dozen Nurses and execute a search for the rogue zombie. Ben will host Monster Trivia in the amphitheater, while Shane stands guard with a few of the karate-trained Nurses. First, however, please allow me to show you to your rooms. You could probably use a shower and a break."

I looked down to see my shirt caked with dried sea worm slime and wet with sweat. I took a whiff of my armpit and nearly passed out.

"Wow," Ben said, looking at his own clothes. "I almost forgot how I got here."

"How did we get here?" asked Gordon. "And where *is* here?"

Our break wasn't long—the Director gave us fifteen minutes. We met in the hallway.

"Whoa!" said Shane, as the door slammed behind him. "Did you see that view!? Amazing!"

"How can you think about the view when there's a deranged zombie on the loose?" asked Ben.

"Look, I know how to handle zombies," said Shane. "Maybe we should enjoy a nice fruit smoothie and kick it on the sand for a bit."

"I hate to break it to you," I said, "but we're not exactly on vacation."

We walked back down to the theater to meet with the Nurses. Shane pulled the karate-trained Nurses to the side.

"Now, this guy is fast, but with no arms and just stubs for feet, his center of gravity is off," said Shane. "Low sweeping kicks will be the easiest way to stop him."

Ben headed down to the stage with Horace. All the monsters gathered in the theater, dressed in relaxing beachwear. They all seemed happy, filled with energy, tanned, and fit. They were still old, but they didn't seem completely incapacitated anymore.

"Chris the Sussoroblat Wrecker! 'Sup, Duder?"

The voice came from behind me. I turned around swiftly and stared at an old but amazingly fit-looking zombie surfer, complete with a surfboard impaled through his body.

"Huh?" I said.

He reached out a rotten green hand that had seaweed strands stuck between its fingers. I gave it a shake.

"Yo," he said, "I'm Clive. Director Z asked me to show you around our facilities."

"I told you the zombies could talk!" Shane said.

“Some of us better than others,” Clive said. “With all the sun and the sea here, and the relaxed lifestyle, I’ve been able to keep in pretty good shape. Maybe all the seawater has pickled my brains!”

“The zombie in the infirmary was talking,” I said. “But, he was so old—how was he able to talk? And he said weird things, like we didn’t matter because we were just young ones.”

Before the zombie surfer could answer, Gordon jumped in.

“Cool,” said Gordon. “Nice surfboard.”

Gordon gave the board a knock and Clive winced.

“Yo, that’s a little sore, dude!” he groaned.

“Sorry!”

“Wait,” said Shane. “Why didn’t you head to Raven Hill with the rest of the residents?”

“We got a pretty good run of waves,” said Clive, “and I was so busy hanging ten that by the time I was done, everyone was gone! When a wipeout can’t kill you, you could just surf forever!”

“But how do you surf with that thing sticking out of you?” asked Gordon.

“It ain’t easy,” said Clive.

“All right,” I said. “Ben’s about to start. Let’s get going.”

I grabbed a few Nurses, gave Shane a thumbs-up, and turned to Clive.

"Okay," I said. "Where should we start?"

"The resort towers are pretty well guarded," Clive said, "so I don't think that the rogue zombie got into those. He's either still in the jungle, on the beach, or at the aquarium."

"Aquarium?" I asked. "Director Z didn't say anything about an aquarium."

"Well, Directors are never going to tell you everything," Clive said. "They've always got something up their sleeves."

"What sort of aquarium?" Gordon asked.

"Aw, it's cool, man!" said Clive. "Like SeaWorld for sea monsters. With all the monster juice drainage, it's hard for some of these creatures to be out in the open ocean anymore."

"Wait, you call lebensplasm *monster juice*?" Gordon asked. "That's what we call it!"

"Yeah, my dude, it's gotta be monster juice! It just sounds so much cooler," said Clive, while high-fiving Gordon.

"Let's start at the aquarium," I said.

"You got it!" said Clive.

SeaMonsterWorld

I thought I knew everything about monsters working at Raven Hill, but then I visited the Paradise Island Aquarium and Sea Creature Rehabilitation Center. We stood in the main entrance—glass walls towered ominously in front of us. Dark figures shifted in the tanks.

"This is freaking me out a little," I said. "How thick is that glass?"

"Forget about the tanks," said Gordon. "That freak could be hiding in here, and it's really dark."

"Yeah, most of these sea monsters prefer the dark," said Clive. "Except for the mermaids. They have a display with big rocks. They like to lay out and catch the rays."

The Nurses handed out flashlights and we turned them on. An ominous glow filled the massive room.

"How should we split up?" I asked Clive.

"Uhhh . . ." Clive scratched his head. A clump of hair and seaweed fell out. "Two Nurses should head down the west wing toward Moby Dick. Two should head toward the sea serpent display—make sure Hydra still has three heads. Two more should go talk with the mermaids and sirens, but DON'T get too close. The three of us will head toward the Kraken."

"You have a Kraken!?" Gordon yelled.

"Moby Dick is real?" I asked.

"Sure," replied Clive. "Vampires are real. I'm real. Why not Moby Dick—one of the fiercest sea monsters?"

"I wonder what other crazy monsters there are in the world," I gasped.

"We've got a couple of the craziest in our collection," Clive continued. "Have you ever seen a vampire squid?"

We headed deeper into the aquarium's main hall. Moans and groans came from the tanks. The hair on the back of my neck slowly rose. I swept my flashlight around the nooks and crannies, waiting for a rogue zombie to pounce, but there was nothing but shadow.

"Maybe we should have brought a Nurse," I said.

"Don't worry, dude," Clive said, "I'll be able to talk him down. Hey, check these guys out." He pointed at a tank to his right.

"What's in there?" Gordon asked.

In a flash, a huge, rotten shark flung itself at us.

THUNK!

"Whaa!" Gordon and I jumped back.

Another shark hit the glass and chomped at us.

The glass shook, but stayed in place.

"Coooool," said Clive. He clapped his hands together.

"What happened to those sharks?" I asked.

"Well, one day I was surfing, and a shark tried to bite me, so I bit him back."

"ZOMBIE SHARKS!?!" said Gordon. "That's amazing!"

"TOTALLY GNARLY, RIGHT!" Clive said, and then high-fived Gordon again. "The first guy went off and bit a few more. They act all aggro, but they're totally chill with humans—all you gotta do is growl at them, and they totally remember who made them zombies."

A long, low growl came from the end of the hallway.

"Whoa," said Clive, "the Kraken is angry. I guess we got too loud. Come on, let's check him out and see if our little rogue friend is down this way."

We walked to the very end of the hallway, and stood in front of the largest tank we had seen so far. Tentacles floated in and out of sight.

"No rogue zombies down here," said Gordon.

"Yeah," I said. "Let's go see if the Nurses found anything."

"Wait a second, dudes," said Clive, pointing to the tank.

A huge eye loomed in front of us, staring us down.

"What's up, big guy?" asked Clive.

The eye blinked once.

"This guy's heavy," Clive said. "He's the strongest sea monster we've got here. His jaw can crush a battleship. He's a little weak, like the rest of us, but he could still do some major damage. I'd like to take him for a ride, but I don't have a strong enough karate chop. One strong whack to the top of the head, and he'll listen to any instruction you give him."

We turned back down the hallway and headed to the entrance.

The Nurses didn't find anything in the aquarium, so we spent the rest of the day searching the jungle and found absolutely nothing. We returned to the resort, where we updated Director Z, Ben, and Shane in the dining room. A chef, who looked exactly like a Nurse except for his uniform, brought over a steaming tray of frog legs.

"Wait," said Ben. "Before I bite into this, I just have to ask: Is it even safe?"

"I assure you, it's been properly prepared," replied Director Z. "Our chefs are quite skilled at dezombification."

"Well, I'm hungry," said Gordon, and he started tearing at the leg meat.

"Eat up, gentlemen," said Director Z. "We have a long night ahead of us. We'll need to keep watch. Please break into shifts. I'll ask the Nurses to do the same, but they're not exactly big on details—they might miss something. I need your eyes out there."

"Well someone else can take the first shift, because I'm exhausted," I said. "I need to sleep for a few hours."

"I'm ON IT!" said Gordon.

"Wow," Shane said. "What did Griselda's spell do to you? You're pumped."

"Thanks, Gordon," I said.

I grabbed a pair of frog legs and stood up.

"I'm pooped. I'll just nibble these in my room, if you guys don't mind," I said.

"Of course," Director Z said. "Good night, Chris. I will also be turning in early tonight. I haven't slept in nearly three days. I'm so glad you gentlemen are here."

"Good night." I yawned.

I shuffled up to my room and passed out.

Romantically Rotten Dinners

"Dude," Gordon yelled, shaking me violently out of a deep sleep. It felt like the island was having an earthquake.

"I gotta sleep," I mumbled and turned over. "I'll pass out tomorrow if I don't."

"C'mon, wake up," he said, shaking me again.

I ignored him and drifted back to sleep. Moments later I awoke with a gasp. Something horribly putrid had filled my lungs. I tried to sit up to but something pinned me down on the bed. As hard as I struggled, I couldn't get to fresh air.

Then I heard what sounded like laughing. I recognized the voice. Gordon had pulled the sheet over my head, slid his butt under it, and farted, sealing me in. It was disgusting—I felt like I had been covered in a layer of fart sweat. My nostrils flared.

"You're sick, dude!" I yelled, finally able to peel the covers off of my face.

"Well, you should have just woken up when I told you to," Gordon said, giggling.

I tried to kick him, but he was already headed through my open door.

"You've got to see this!" he yelled. "This is hilarious."

With an angry grunt, I kicked off the stinky sheet and followed him outside.

I was happy to be breathing in the hot, heavy, moist air. In the starry, cloudless sky above, an almost-full moon shined. It was so clear, you could almost make out the moon's face—a combination of plains, highlands, and craters that made the moon look like it had eyes, a nose, and a mouth. I sighed, remembering how close I was to touching moon rock at Kennedy Space Center.

Still half asleep, I asked Gordon, "Are you showing me the moon?"

"Naw, stupid," he said. "What I'm about to show you, ya don't see every day. Keep walking. Shane and Ben are already there."

I shuffled down a shorter path than the one we had used earlier in the day, and came out on the beach. At the very end of the beach, up against the cliffs, loomed a massive dead whale.

"Ha-ha," I said, and yawned. "That beached whale is really funny, Gordon! The way its body has rotted and hollowed out to show its ribs. HILARIOUS!"

I turned around to leave, but Gordon grabbed me.

"Just wait until we get closer," he said, and chuckled.

We walked farther down the beach, and found Shane and Ben crouched behind a huge pile of driftwood.

"Get down," they hissed as we approached.

"They're too busy staring in each other's eyes to notice us," Gordon said.

"Who?!" I asked. Now I was really interested.

Gordon and I crouched down behind the driftwood with our friends. Our four heads peeked up over the wood and stared at the beached whale. It took a while for my eyes to adjust, but then I saw it.

"No way!" I said. "Clarice and Pietro are having dinner in the whale carcass."

"Yep, they sure are," said Gordon, and he had to put his hand over his mouth to stifle a giggle.

"I mean, this is serious," said Shane. "They must have snuck out after lights-out. They've got the checkered tablecloth and a nice candelabra. They've got really beautiful plates and silverware. Well done, Pietro!"

They sat at a small table inside the whale carcass. Pietro, the werewolf, picked up his fork, speared something on his plate, and then reached over to feed it to Clarice, the banshee.

She plucked the morsel off of the fork with her teeth, and began to chew delicately.

"What are they eating?" I asked.

"I think they're eating the whale," Ben said. "It must have washed up on the beach a few weeks ago. That thing is STINKY."

Just as Ben finished his statement, a strong wind blew up the beach, and we could smell the rotting sea creature.

"Ugggh," I said, and covered my nose.

"Wait, look," said Shane. "Ben is right!"

Pietro, huge butcher knife in hand, stood up, walked deeper into the whale, grabbed a nice rotten chunk, and sliced it off. He brought it down on the platter between their plates. He reached up and grabbed a scoop of the fat that was dripping off the rib cage above them, putting it on the whale meat like one would put whipped cream on an ice cream sundae.

"Banshees eat whale, huh? Who'd have known?" asked Gordon.

"Love makes you do strange things," said Ben with a sigh.

"Shut up, guys," I said. "I think they're talking."

It was hard to hear because of the shifting winds. We cupped our ears.

"When I first heard you screech at Raven Hill," said Pietro, "my ears perked right up. I knew that yours was the voice I always wanted howling at the moon with me."

"Oh, Pietro," purred the banshee, "you're just too kind. Well, I love that you actually still have all that hair on your head—most of the men around here are bald as babies!"

She reached up to his bushy head and started to twirl his hair.

His leg started twitching like a dog's.

"So silky," she said. "Do you use conditioner?"

"He most certainly does not," said Shane. "But he does like to roll around in dead things."

I started to laugh uncontrollably. Ben and Gordon soon followed.

We tried hard to stop, for fear of being heard, but it was too late.

Pietro stood up . . . and looked right at us.

"What are you doing here?" he asked.

We slunk lower behind the driftwood.

The vegetation next to us started to rustle, and out stepped another werewolf—I think his name was Howie. He held an accordion.

"What am I doing here?" he said. "You said ten o'clock, right?"

"Yes, and it's nine thirty," said Pietro. "We haven't even finished our main course."

"Forget it then," Howie said, "I'll just transform and

find something to roll around in for a while."

He was about to put the accordion down when Clarice stood up.

"No, wait," she said. "I'd love some music."

"Wonderful, then!" said Howie.

He started to play a crazy tune on the accordion, and the banshee nodded her head in appreciation. The song continued for a few seconds and then Howie started to sing.

"Awooo, awooo, aweeeeeeeoooo," Howie howled.

Pietro and Clarice joined in, their howls and screeches rattling the whale ribs.

"Man," said Gordon, "this is crazy."

We all plugged our ears while the three kept screeching and howling.

When the music was over, Clarice and Pietro began applauding wildly.

"Bravo, BRAVO!" she said.

"Well," Howie said with a bow, "I'll leave you two alone now. Have a wonderful evening!"

"Thanks, Howie," said Pietro. "I really, really appreciate it, my brother. Sorry I got snippy before."

Howie slunk back into the brush, leaving Pietro and Clarice in the moonlight.

"That was so romantic," said Clarice, and she put her head on Pietro's shoulder.

"Well," said Pietro, putting his hand around her back,

"now that we've had dinner and some entertainment, perhaps we should have a little dessert."

"Oh, my," she said. "What do you have for dessert?"

"Just your sweet, sweet lips," said Pietro.

"Oooh, not smooth," said Shane.

Clarice lifted her head in surprise.

The both moved in closer for a kiss.

"Ewww," said Gordon. "This is going to be gross."

They moved even closer . . .

. . . when a splash made us turn our heads. It sounded like something had flopped up onto the beach, but I couldn't see anything. Pietro and Clarice clearly didn't notice, as they were still lost in their kiss.

"Ewww," said Gordon again. "Old people kissing is just so gross."

"I think it's beautiful," said Shane. "Cross-monster relationships. We're entering a new era."

"Whatever," said Gordon.

"AAAAAHHHHHHHH!"

A screech pierced our ears.

"You bit me," said Clarice, jumping up from her seat. "And I thought you were a gentleman!"

She got up to leave, and Pietro got up to follow.

"Wait! I'm a werewolf, and you taste good! I had a moment of weakness! It will never happen again! Wait!"

"This was a huge mistake," she said.

Pietro suddenly dropped to the ground, shaking and drooling.

"Pietro?! PIETRO!?" Clarice yelled.

"Guurrrrggggllllyyyaaaaaah!" Pietro was struggling with something invisible, his arms pinned to his side, his head twisted back in agony.

"What the heck?" said Ben.

We jumped up and ran over toward Pietro.

Clarice saw us and said, "I have no idea what happened. It came on so quick!"

Shane leaned down to help Pietro up, but he thrashed around violently, frothing at the mouth.

"Pietro!" Shane yelled. "Relax!"

Pietro howled, and Shane jumped back.

"He won't bite you," I said.

"No, it's not that," said Shane. "Something's covering him. A thin skin."

"What!?" said Clarice.

Pietro thrashed and kicked the sand, fighting some invisible assailant. He growled and snapped his teeth.

"It's disappeared," said Shane, "but it was there when he howled."

"Howl again!" I yelled. "Pietro, howl again!"

"Aaaaarrrooooooooo!" Pietro howled, and the skin lifted off his body again, but sucked tight against him as soon as he was done howling.

"Again," Clarice yelled. "AAAAGGGAAIIINNNNN!"

“Your scream is helping,” said Shane to Clarice.

“Arrrrooooooooooooooooaaaaahhhhh!” we all yelled as a clear skin peeled itself off Pietro, from his feet up to his forehead, with a wet, sticky sound.

The skin slowly rolled off of his head, and Pietro stopped struggling and started shaking. The skin was barely visible—almost completely see-through.

“Grab it,” Ben yelled.

Gordon pounced, but by the time he hit the ground, all that was left was sand.

The skin zoomed back to the water, and with a splash it was gone.

“What *was* that thing?!” screeched Ben.

“Pietro, are you okay?” Clarice knelt down next to Pietro.

“He looks like he’s twenty years older,” I said.

“I . . . feel . . . twenty years . . . older,” he said, and then turned into an old mangy dog.

Old mangy Pietro laid in the sand, sleeping and dreaming, his paws twitching uneasily.

“We should bring him back up to the facility,” I said.

I've Got You Under My Skin

Gordon picked up the twitching dog and we all headed up the nearest path to the resort.

"It'll be all right, Pietro," said Gordon. "We're gonna get you some help."

Halfway to the resort, we ran into Director Z. His fine silk pajamas flapped in the ocean breeze.

"I heard screams and came as quickly as I could," he said. "What is it?"

"It's Pietro," I said. "He's been attacked by a weird sea skin."

"It covered him and drained him insanely fast," said Shane. "I think this is why the other residents are sick."

“Are you sure this skin is actually gone?” Director Z asked.

“Yeah, we heard it splash back into the ocean,” said Gordon.

Two Nurses pounded down the path toward us.

“Nurse Inx,” commanded Director Z, “take Pietro to the infirmary as swiftly as you can. Nurse Glick, raise the witches—we’ll need special potions to be brewed tonight.”

The Nurses ran off.

“Clarice,” said the Director, “what on Earth were you doing outside? Why did you and Pietro violate our curfew?”

“I know, I know,” said Clarice. “It was a very stupid thing to do.”

“What is that on your lip?” asked Director Z. “Were you bitten by the sea skin?”

“Well . . . no.” She hesitated. “It wasn’t the sea skin . . .”

There was a long silence.

“Very well,” said Director Z.

Clarice went back to her room. Director Z turned to us.

“Gentlemen, this is quite a development. We should all meet in my office. Please just give me fifteen minutes to ready myself, and do grab Clive. He’s in room 345.”

Director Z stormed back up the path.

Fifteen minutes later, we arrived at Director Z's office with Clive. A broken fish tank sat to the right of a huge desk. I walked over to the massive tank—the front of the tank was smashed in and the tank was completely dry. A small brass plate attached to the wood under the tank read PYGOCENTRUS NATTERERI.

I was about to ask Director Z what that meant when he sat down behind his desk. The desk still had a HERR DIREKTOR DETLEF nameplate sitting on it.

"Gentlemen," he said, "please do have a seat."

There was a leather couch and plush chairs surrounding a rug in front of the desk. We all chose a spot and sat down.

"Ummm, Boss . . ." Clive was halfway into his seat, and the board that ran through his body wouldn't let him go any further.

"I think I'll just stand," he said.

"That's quite fine," said Director Z. "Tell me, have you ever seen or heard about the bizarre skin creature that attacked Pietro?"

"No, I can't say that I have," replied Clive. "Totally new to me."

"I've been trying to ask Herr Direktor Detlef about it," said Director Z, "but I can't reach him at his number, and nobody seems to be picking up the phone at Raven Hill."

"Should we be worried?" Ben asked.

"Possibly," said Director Z, "but let's focus on the problem at hand. First, how can we be sure that this skin creature is responsible for all of the lebensplasm loss on the island?"

"I think it *has* to be," I said. "Each of the sick residents was drained extremely fast—just like Pietro."

"And," said Shane, "each of the sick residents was sealed in. We saw fluids from the monsters ooze out, but stay pressed against their bodies."

"And we couldn't even get lebensplasm levels," said Director Z. "But why do the victims act so strangely, so wild?"

"The skin must control them somehow," said Ben.

"What else do we know?" Director Z asked.

"Well," said Gordon, "it came from the ocean. We heard a splash as it came out of the water, and another splash when it went back in."

"We know it drained Pietro," said Shane, "but it was never able to control him. He was able to howl the skin off. Maybe it takes time to seal?"

"So, in essence, we're dealing with a deadly skin from the ocean that can seal itself perfectly onto its victim's body, drain the victim's lebensplasm, and control the victim. We're dealing with multiple skins, and the skins can't be removed by any means but howling."

"Yes," said Shane, "although I'm not sure how much time you would have to howl it off once it attacks. Maybe only ten or fifteen seconds."

"What else, gentlemen, what else?" asked a frustrated Director Z. "We must learn more about these beasts. But how?"

"We could ask the possessed monsters a series of questions," said Ben, "and see if we could get the right answers, or at least clues."

"I have a better idea," I said. "Let's follow the skin into the ocean and see where it goes—maybe learn something about it. Or catch it and bring it back to study it. Is this island equipped with a lab?"

"Yes, this island houses a premier lebensplasm research facility. But how are we going to get a skin to go back into the ocean?" Director Z asked.

"We just need to re-create the events of tonight," I replied.

"Clarice and Pietro need to kiss again?" Gordon asked. "Ewww."

"Clarice and Pietro were kissing?" Director Z asked.

"Well," said Ben, "they ended with a kiss. But there was a lot that lead up to it—a romantic candlelight dinner. An accordion song. And then there's the bite."

"The bite?" Director Z asked. "Oh . . . the mark on Clarice's lips . . ."

"If we re-create the date in every detail," I continued, "at the very same time it happened tonight, there may be a chance that the same skin will come for Pietro."

"Only this time when he howls it off," Shane said, "we go after it! Genius!"

"But how?" Gordon said. "Are we just going to throw on wet suits and swim really fast?"

"We've actually got some really gnarly scuba gear," said Clive. "And it's brand-new! None of the monsters use it, since most of them don't need to breathe underwater—or at all—but I think that should work."

"And do you have anything that could be used as transportation?" Director Z asked Clive.

"Yeah," Clive said. "Zombie sharks."

"Come again?" asked Director Z, eyebrow raised.

"Zombie sharks," Clive said, laughing. "They're a lot less deadly than they sound. In fact, zombie sharks are pretty chill around humans, because it was a human zombie that turned them into zombie sharks. *This* human zombie, to be precise."

"How do we get them to move?" asked Ben. "How do we steer them?"

"It's simple," said Clive. "You just dangle a little brain in front of them, and *zoom*, they're off. Need to turn right? Just dangle the brain a bit to the right. Need to turn left? Just—"

"We get the idea," Ben said. "But where are you

planning on getting the . . . um . . . brains for the mission?"

"Your friend Chris tells me that you're pretty smart," said Clive. "We could use your brains."

"See, this is what happens when you study," said Gordon.

"Naw, man," chuckled Clive. "I'm just kidding. We can just use some vegetable brain."

"Vegetable brain?" Shane asked.

"Yeah, man!" said Clive. "But it's really a fruit."

"Wait . . . ," I said, trying to clear my head. "Let me get this straight. The zombie sharks are going to chase down a fruit just because it's called *vegetable brain*?"

"They don't call it vegetable brain for nothin'!" said Clive.

"Vegetable brain . . . ," Ben mumbled as he pulled out his phone. "I really wish I could Google that, but there's no service on this island."

"Well, then, it's settled," said Director Z. "I'll send some nurses into the jungle to collect enough vegetable brain for the purpose. Chris, please work with Pietro and Clarice to make sure that tonight's date can be re-created. Clive, if you could please show the gentlemen how to work with the zombie sharks?"

Free Shark Rides for the Kids!

That next morning we waited nervously on top of the zombie sharks' tank for our riding lessons.

"I hope Clive's a no-show," said Ben. "I threw up on a plane; I don't think my stomach can handle riding a zombie shark. And what if they try to eat *our* brains?"

"I don't know," Gordon replied. "I'm kind of looking forward to it. This is like the ultimate extreme sport."

Gordon and Shane high-fived.

"Here he comes now," I said, and pointed to Clive dragging a bunch of scuba gear up the stairs to the top of the tank.

"Sorry I'm late, dudes," said Clive.

We all squeezed into our gear.

“Ummm . . .” Ben said. “Guys? I can’t really see.”

We looked over to see Ben’s helmet fogged up.

“It’s really hot in here,” he said. “I’m not so worried about the zombie shark anymore. I’m worried I’m going to barf in *here* first. GUYS!?! ARE YOU THERE?!?”

“Deep breaths, dude,” said Clive. “Just chill.”

Gordon was stretching his suit out by running to the water’s edge and back.

Suddenly the water at the top of the tank exploded and four rotten sharks flopped onto the platform right in front of Gordon.

“Ah!” yelled Ben as he fell over. “What the heck is going on?”

The sharks flopped and shook in the open air, but were able to turn teeth-side toward Gordon.

“Clive?” screamed Gordon, who was too stunned to move. “CLIVE?!”

The shark closest to Gordon used his fins to push himself forward. He opened his massive mouth wide, but before it could bite down on Gordon, Clive jumped into its mouth and . . .

CHOMP!

His surfboard pinned the shark’s mouth open.

“Right on time, you stank fishies,” yelled Clive. “Now, you better behave, or Daddy’s gonna bite your nosies!”

The shark let Clive go and backed down. The other three started to whimper and shake.

“That’s what I THOUGHT,” yelled Clive. He grabbed the shark that had just bit him by the gill. “You! Stay here.”

Clive turned to us. “Who’s ready to rock?”

“CHRIS IS,” my three friends said and pointed at me. They had clearly planned for this moment.

“Dude,” said Clive, “come on over.”

I slowly approached the shark. Its bloodshot eye turned toward me and it opened its mouth with a growl.

“Stop that!” yelled Clive, and gave the shark’s nose a good slap.

Clive started the lesson. “All right, Chris. First thing you need to do is growl at the shark as you walk up to it. He needs to know you mean business.”

“Grrr,” I said.

“More,” said Clive.

“GRRR,” I said.

“Mean it,” said Clive. “All you need to do is scare him, and he’ll do whatever you want.”

“GRRRRRRRRRRRR!”

The shark started to shake.

“Awesome, dude!” said Clive. “Now get on top of him and grab his fin!”

I looked at my friends.

“Go for it!” said Shane.

I mounted the shark, who growled and bucked below me.

"GRAB THE FIN, DUDE!" yelled Clive.

"Whoa," I said, clutching the fin. "Whoa, sharkie!"

"Kick his side!" yelled Clive. "Show him who's boss!"

I couldn't believe what I was doing. I thought of the rodeo I had seen a few years ago, and kicked the shark in the side while pulling back on his fin.

The shark stopped.

"Great!" Clive said. He dug around in a bag and pulled out a fishing pole. Hanging off the line was a piece of something yellowish-white and wrinkly. "Here's your vegetable brain. Just hold it in the direction you want to go, and go!"

I grabbed the fishing pole and dangled it in front of the shark. He started to creep forward, his fins flopping on the wet platform.

"Okay," I said, as the shark started to tip into the tank. I was frightened and excited. "Here I go! Yee-haw!"

The shark tipped over—SPLASH—and took off!

He was extremely fast, and extremely strong. I desperately clutched his fin with my left hand. I tried my best to wriggle the vegetable brain in a way that would get him to swim straight, but he was spiraling down to the bottom of the tank, shooting back up, swimming all over the place.

"Aaaahhhhhhh!" I screamed.

Only twenty seconds in the tank, and I didn't know which way was up. The shark jerked to the right and I felt the pole slip out of my hand. He bucked up, and I felt myself fly—first through the water, and then through air.

I landed with an OOF. Through my water-streaked helmet, I could see the other three sharks in front of me.

"Grr," I said weakly. The world spun before me. I felt like every part of my body was vibrating.

"You should be stoked," said Clive, who helped me up. "That was a great first run! We gotta work on some stuff here and there, but that was awesome! Who's next?"

I slowly made my way down the spiral staircase to the benches in front of the huge window looking into the tank. I sat down and closed my eyes to collect myself for a few minutes. I opened them up to see a zombie shark fling Shane against the window. He gave me a thumbs-up as he slowly slid down the glass.

This was going to take all day.

Date Night Re-do

Later that night, we were exhausted and sore, but ready to ride. Gordon, Shane, Ben, and I all stood behind the same piece of driftwood that we had the night before—this time in scuba gear. Just two hundred feet behind us, Clive held on tightly to the zombie sharks in preparation for our voyage.

"This is absolutely crazy," said Ben.

"I think that's why I like it," Shane said.

"You know who really thinks this is crazy?" I asked.

"Who?" asked Gordon.

"Clarice!" I replied. "The poor woman is sick of Pietro, but she's agreed to go through everything that happened last night, from appetizers to being bitten."

"She's getting nipped by an old werewolf," Gordon said. "We're riding zombie sharks into the deep. Now you tell me who's in for a crazier night."

A figure came shuffling up the beach to us. It was hard to tell who it was, even in the moonlight.

"Wait," the figure huffed, "I'm ready! Director Z said I should help you kids out!"

"Gil?" Ben asked, "Is that you?"

Sure enough, the old swamp creature shuffled up to us, huffing and puffing.

"I'm better at swimming than running," he said.

"Why are you wearing scuba gear?" asked Gordon. "Aren't you a fish?"

"I'm a freshwater fish," said the swamp creature. "This water is far too salty for me. But I know I'll be able to help you down there."

"Wow," said Shane, "a fish in scuba gear. Cool."

"All right," I said, "just crouch down with us behind this log, and stay quiet. No swamp gas."

"No swamp gas, got it," the swamp creature agreed.

Up ahead, Pietro and Clarice approached the whale carcass.

"Just get this straight," Clarice said to Pietro. "This is NOT going anywhere. I'm only doing this to help everyone out."

"Clarice, honey—" Pietro started.

"Don't 'honey' me!" Clarice yelled back.

I popped up from behind the driftwood, and yelled, "Guys! This is serious! You have to do everything exactly as you did before. You weren't yelling at each other!"

"Now *you're* yelling," pointed out Shane.

"Just this once," I hissed at him.

I crouched back down behind the driftwood with my friends and the swamp creature. Our five heads peeked up over the wood and stared at the beached whale. We waited five or ten minutes, while Clarice and Pietro ate their appetizers quietly.

"Okay, this is about the time we started talking," I said.

"I said something like, 'Wow, they snuck out. Pietro did a great job with the checkered tablecloth and plates and everything,'" said Shane.

Pietro picked up his fork, speared something on his plate, and then reached over to feed it to Clarice.

She grabbed the wad of whale flesh and stuffed it in her mouth.

"But you ate it off the fork before," Pietro whined.

"I'm telling you, thish ish going nowhere," said Clarice with a mouth full of whale flesh. "Thish ish absolutely dishgusting, by the way."

"I said something like, 'What are they eating,'" I said.

"And I said, 'They're eating the stinky whale, blah, blah, blah," said Ben.

"Blah, blah, blah," said Gordon.

"Blah, blah, blah," said Shane.

"Blah, blah, blah," said the swamp creature.

"Shush," I said to the swamp creature. "You weren't here."

The swamp creature shushed, and we all peeked over the log to Pietro and Clarice.

"When I first heard you screech at Raven Hill," said Pietro, "my ears perked right up. I knew that yours was the voice I always wanted howling at the moon with me."

"Oh, Pietro," said the banshee through clenched teeth. "You're. Just. Too. Kind. Ugh, I can't take this. Your hair is greasy and smells like cat turds. How you found a litter box to roll around in at Paradise Island is beyond me."

She reached up to his bushy head with a BLECH and started to twirl his hair.

His leg started twitching like a dog's.

"Then came Shane's joke and we started to laugh," I said.

"Har har har huh huh huh," we all fake-laughed.

Pietro stood up . . .

"What are you doing here?" he asked.

The vegetation next to us started to rustle, and out stepped Howie. He held his accordion.

"Yeah, what am I doing here?" he asked. "I thought

you said Clarice and you were through."

"And I think we still are," Pietro said. "But we still need to do this. I told you."

Howie played his crazy tune and the three of them howled. The whale's exposed ribs rattled again, though not quite as hard as the night before.

"I hope this works," I said.

When the music was over, Clarice and Pietro applauded.

"Bravo," she said, with no emotion at all.

"I'm outta here," said Howie.

"Thanks, Howie," said Pietro.

Howie slunk back into the brush, leaving Pietro and Clarice alone in the moonlight.

"I can't believe I'm doing this," said Clarice, and she put her head on Pietro's shoulder.

"Well," said Pietro putting his hand around her back, "now that we've had dinner—"

"Yeah, yeah," she said. "What do you have for dessert?"

"Just your sweet, sweet lips," said Pietro.

"Oooh, not smooth, Pietro," said Clarice.

Clarice lifted her head. They both moved in closer for the kiss.

"Ewww," mumbled Clarice. "This is going to be gross."

They moved even closer . . .

SPLASH!

"Yessss!" I hissed.

Gordon was still staring at the kiss.

"I've said it before, and I'll say it again," he said. "Old people kissing is gross."

"I think it's so sad it didn't work out," said Shane. "This could have been an amazing cross-monster relationship. Gil, are you currently looking for love? I hear Griselda's single."

"I've always been partial to Queen Hatshepsut," said the swamp creature.

"Ahhh, so you're a mummy man, eh?" said Shane.

"Shhhh," I said. "Get ready."

"AAAAAHHHHHHHH!"

The screech pierced our ears!

"I can't believe I let you bite me again," said Clarice, jumping up from her seat.

She got up to leave, and Pietro got up to follow.

"Wait! Wait! I really think we can work this out."

"This was a huge mistake," she said.

Pietro dropped to the ground, shaking and drooling.

"Goooooooo!" I yelled.

We ran down to the water and the zombie sharks.

"Take it easy down there," said Clive. "I wish I could come with you, but I do nothing but float with this surfboard crammed into me. Reserve your energy. Don't get gassed out too quick!"

We mounted our sharks and put on our helmets. Shane's shark had a small pouch strapped to it. Inside the pouch was a net.

"Let's hope we're lucky enough to catch this thing," I said.

Clive ran up to each shark and turned on the headlamps he had strapped on them. As he turned each light on, he yelled in the shark's ears.

"Don't try anything funny down there," he yelled, "or the humans riding on you will bite you into bits."

We all growled, and the sharks shuddered.

"Now, follow the brains!" Clive said, and we held up our vegetable brains.

Howling and screeching came from the whale carcass.

"There it is!" yelled Gordon.

In the moonlight, we could see the sea skin slink down to the water's edge.

"Gooooooo!" I yelled.

We kicked our sharks and wiggled our vegetable brains.

The last thing I heard as we crashed under the waves was "Good luck!" from Clive.

Ripped from the Deep!

Our four zombie sharks swam deeper. The swamp creature kept pace alongside us. At first, I couldn't see anything through the murky water. Between the waves and trying to steer the zombie sharks in the open ocean, I was worried we had lost the skin.

I opened up my helmet communicator.

"Testing, testing, one, two, three," I said. "Are you getting this?"

"Copy," said Ben.

"Copy," said Gordon.

"Copy that," said Shane.

BLLLUUUURRRFFT!

"What was that?" Gordon asked.

"Sorry," said the swamp creature. "I held in a lot of swamp gas up on the beach." FFFFLLLLAAAARRRT!

"Fine," I said. "We can't breathe it in down here, anyway."

We had finally got out of the murky water created by the waves, and could see a coral reef below us.

"Get your sharks to move their headlamps around," I said. "We have to find this thing!"

Fish shot out of the way of the zombie sharks as we skimmed the top of the coral reef. Crabs scuttled for shelter.

"This is beautiful," said Ben. "So many colors."

"Oh, suuuuuuuuuuure," said the swamp creature. "Everybody loves a coral reef. But a swamp . . . that's a beautiful thing."

We circled around the area where we though the skin had gone, and then circled around it again.

"I think we've lost it," said Shane.

"Wait!" said Gordon. "Follow me! I see something shimmering ahead."

Gordon kicked his zombie shark and shot forward. We followed.

"He's right," said Shane. "I can see it up there!"

"Whoa!" yelled Gordon and stopped his shark.

"What's going on?" I asked as we reached Gordon.

"Oh . . . ," said Ben, pointing down.

Gordon had stopped at the edge of a huge drop.

Behind us was the colorful, lively reef. Below us were dark, cloudy waters. We could see the skin slowly slink deeper and deeper until it was lost in the dark.

"I wonder how far down it goes?" Ben asked.

"I'm not sure," I replied, "but we *have* to go after it."

"All right, boss," said Shane.

"I dunno, guys," said Ben. "This is pretty creepy."

A high-pitched screech floated up from the deep.

"Let's go," said the swamp creature.

We headed down into the deep.

"I can barely see in front of me," Gordon said, "it's so murky."

"And fr-fr-freezing," stuttered Ben.

The sharks plodded ahead, and soon their headlamps gleamed off the skin.

"It's right in front of us," Gordon said.

"We've reached the bottom of this trench," I said, and shined my light along the lifeless sea floor. "Look."

"Oh, man," said Ben. "Take a look at this."

He shined his light on something white lying on the floor.

"Is that a skeleton?" I asked

"Yep," said Shane. "A human skeleton."

"Oh, man," I said. "This isn't good."

"Um, guys," said Gordon, "check this out."

He had stopped his zombie shark. The shark's headlamp shined on a wicked looking monster that bloomed out of a huge fleshy sea pod like a sick flower. Its face looked like an eel's, razor-sharp teeth lined its mouth, and its hands were massive crab claws. Huge bloody gills breathed in and out. Below the scaly, slimy neck, the creature's organs hung out freely, bobbing around in the shifting waters.

"What the heck?!" Ben said.

"Membranium!" said the swamp creature.

"What?" said Gordon.

"Just watch the skin," said the swamp creature.

The skin floated over to the disgusting creature, and covered it from head to toe. As it did, the skin went from translucent to the same green, scaly, slimy color of the rest of the creature.

"I've heard about these things," said the swamp creature, sounding a little scared now, "but I never knew they ate lebensplasm."

The skin sealed up with a nice PLOP, and the creature opened its eyes.

"Move your lights away," I hissed.

Everyone did as they were told, and swung their sharks around . . .

. . . to reveal an entire wall of membranium! Some had skin, and some did not. Their disgusting bodies swayed in the soft current.

"We've got to get out of here," said the swamp creature, "and we can if we just move fast enough."

"All right," I said. "Everybody—"

"Arrgghh! It's got me," yelled the swamp creature.

He thrashed in the water, screamed . . . and farted.

FRRRRRRRTTTTT!

He stopped thrashing.

"Gil?" I said, "Are you okay?"

"I think so," he said. "Look . . ."

Before the swamp creature could say anything else, my zombie shark bucked from under me. It must have caught a smell of the organs that were floating out in the water, because it headed for the nearest skinless membranium and . . .

CHOMP!!!

The entire wall erupted in screams. The skinless membranium floated in place, but the ones with skins pulled themselves slowly out of their sea pods, and slinked slowly toward us.

"They can only go so far," said the swamp creature. "They're attached by umbilical cords!"

My shark had been bitten by several membranium and was being munched on the wall. I grabbed on to the tail of Ben's zombie shark.

"Swim up, up, uuuuup!" I yelled.

The swamp creature floated up, and Ben, Shane, and Gordon jiggled their vegetable brains in front of their sharks.

But it was too late.

"Skins!" Gordon yelled.

"They're after the zombie sharks!" I said.

Within seconds, three skins had sealed themselves around our zombie sharks. The sharks struggled in the water. The membranium kept coming out of the wall, snarling and snapping, their razor teeth lashing in the water. Their bodies pulsated with anger in the deep water as they released more and more of their umbilical cords.

"We've got to get out of here!" I yelled. "Swim up as fast as you can—they're going to turn the zombie sharks on us!"

We swam as hard as we could, the zombie sharks struggling below us, lashing and snapping at the skin that was closing in on them.

"Grrrrr . . ." They growled and fought. We were halfway up the trench, gaining speed. Then, from the deep—

BLLLLUUUURRRFFFTTTT!

BRRRRRPPPFFFFFT!

SPPPLLUUUUUFFFFFTTTT!

"The sharks just farted," said Shane. "They're turning our way."

We neared the top of the trench, and the sharks were already halfway up. The swamp creature was nowhere to be seen.

"Gil!" I yelled. "We could really use your help!!!"

A huge boulder on the edge of the trench started to shimmy and shake.

"Hurrrrryyyyy," said the swamp creature.

"He's the one pushing the boulder!" yelled Ben.

We shot up past the boulder, and as soon as we leveled off to head for the coral, it tipped over the edge. There were scrapes and crunches as it headed down the side of the trench.

"Hurry," said the swamp creature. "It will just stun them momentarily. You've got to get to the shore. Pull off your gear, you'll float up faster!"

Before the swamp creature could even finish his statement, we each took huge breaths, pulled off our scuba gear, and raced to the surface of the water.

When we burst through the waves, it looked like the beach was at least a hundred yards away. We swam as fast as we could.

"I . . . ," gasped Ben, "I . . . can't do it . . ."

"Yeah," I gasped, "I think I'm done for."

The swamp creature popped up out of the water and grabbed Ben. Shane and Gordon each grabbed one of my arms.

"Let's goooooo!" screamed Gordon.

We swam like crazy, but there was a splash just behind us. The zombie sharks jumped out of the water, belly flopped, and headed for us.

"We're fish food!" yelled Ben.

"Not today!"

"Clive?" I asked.

Sure enough, Clive was using the surfboard lodged in his body to paddle out past us and toward the sharks.

"Hey, you overgrown guppies!" yelled Clive. "Stop this right now, or Daddy's gonna poke your eyes out!"

"Wait," I yelled. "Clive, they're possessed!"

But it was too late.

A shark picked Clive up by his surfboard and whipped his jaw back and forth. Clive flew right off and disappeared under the water. The sharks followed.

"No!!!!" I yelled.

I tried to swim back, but the swamp creature stopped me.

"Are you crazy?" he asked "Do you want to die, too?"

I stopped fighting, and we swam the last ten yards or so to the shore. We flopped up on the beach, breathing hard.

Two waves later, Clive's surfboard washed up next to us.

I passed out.

With a Little Help from an Enemy

I awoke to find myself lying on the cold, wet beach. Under the light of the moon, Director Z leaned over me. Behind him were Shane, Ben, Gordon, and the swamp creature. I looked up and down the beach, but it was just the four of them.

"Clive?" I asked.

"I'm sorry Chris, but we don't think he made it," Director Z said.

"Man, that stinks," I said.

"He totally saved us," said Shane. "He was a good zombie."

"How long was I out?" I asked, standing up.

"Just long enough for Director Z to get down here," Ben said.

"Gil tells me that he knows what's lurking down there," said Director Z.

"Well," said the swamp creature. "I heard rumors before. Rumors about the membranium. Disgusting, grotesque creatures, bound to the seafloor by their own flesh and unable to ever free themselves. To feed, they peel off their own skin, which is then sent to hunt down prey. Once it finds its meal, the skin wraps around the poor soul and slowly drains the life out it. I never knew it had a taste for lebensplasm. And I certainly never heard of the skin controlling its victims."

"So, basically, we now have our answer," said Director Z. "The reason that the residents have been so ill—and so possessed—is because of the hive of membranium that live just off the shore."

"Have you ever heard of these things?" Ben asked Director Z. "Do you know how to defeat them?"

"There is absolutely no research on membranium," said Director Z. "So, figuring out how to defeat them is not going to be easy."

A great gurgling interrupted our conversation. We looked to see the ocean frothing and bubbling at about the spot where the trench was. The water rippled and slowly headed toward the shore.

"Oh no," said the Director.

"The membranium!" said the swamp creature.

"They must be really angry," said Gordon.

The swamp creature farted again.

"I'm sorry," he said. "When I get frightened, I fart."

"Is there ever an occasion where you don't break wind?" asked Director Z, waving his hand in front of his nose. "Wait . . . why don't I smell anything?"

"Well," said the swamp creature, "I'm still locked into this skin. It's not doing anything to me. But, I'm stuck."

"Wait," I said, "it didn't just fall off when you farted in the ocean?"

"No, in fact it gave me the strength I needed to push that boulder onto the sharks."

"But you're not possessed?" asked Shane.

"Nope," said the swamp creature. "Feel great."

The pack of membranium skin was about fifty yards from the shore.

"Wait," Shane said. "Wait a minute. I think I've got a big idea here. I think farting is the answer."

"What do you mean!?" I said. "Shane, be quick and be clear. We don't have much time!"

"When did the zombie sharks fall under the control of the skin?" Shane asked, and then answered his own question, "Right after they farted. And when did the rogue zombie go rogue? Right after it farted."

"Okay, go on . . ." Gordon said. He looked nervously at the membranium skin, which was riding a wave on its way up to the shore.

Shane took in a big breath, and said, "I think that to control their victims, the membranium squeeze them so hard that they fart. That's how the skin knows it's got you! But when the victim farts before the membranium really has a grip on them, then it just stops and sits there."

"That's wonderful for someone like Gil," said Director Z, "but what about the residents who are already affected?"

The first of the skin creatures washed up on the shore, and started creeping up the beach.

"Wait! Remember when the rogue zombie was force-fed herbs?" I asked.

"Yes," everyone said in unison.

"The membranium lost control for just a little bit," I said. "The skin let loose for ten or fifteen seconds. If we could get the monsters to fart just then, they should be okay."

"All right," said Director Z, and then he called up the beach, "all Nurses, this is an ALARM! Please secure the residents in their rooms and await further instructions in the infirmary. Gil, I'll need your help with the victims—you'll make the perfect flatulence coach."

"How can we help? By stopping the line of membranium skin heading into the resort?" I asked.

"No," said Director Z. "I'd rather you remain worthless."

"Worthless!?" yelled Gordon. "We almost lost *our* skin down there."

"No, you misunderstand," said Director Z. "So far the membranium haven't paid you much notice—perhaps they've developed a taste for the residents. But now that you've snooped around their lair, they might have started noticing you."

"Got it," said Shane. "Just tell us what to do."

"I need you to figure out how we can defeat these nasty creatures. Getting the residents to fart, if we can even keep them conscious long enough to, is going to be tough. We need a real solution."

"Got it!" I said.

"For now," said Director Z, watching the last of the membranium head through the jungle, "I'll get Griselda to make as much herbal remedy as possible, and add a gas-producing ingredient. We'll have to hope that we can convince the residents to fart in the ten to fifteen seconds we have when they're released from the membranium's grip."

Director Z ran up the beach, as the sound of screams rose into the air once again.

"GET THEM IN THEIR ROOOOOOMMMMS!" Director Z yelled up to the resort.

I shook my head, trying to stay conscious.

"I'm so overwhelmed," I said.

"We can think this through," said Ben.

Another scream tore through our ears. It started healthy and young, and ended old and garbled.

"Maybe we should let all of the membranium skins attach to monsters," said Gordon, "and then, while they're busy, lead the Kraken down there and POW!"

"It's a good idea," I said, "but did you see how many membranium there were down there? We'd need three or four times more monsters."

"Plus," added Shane, "what if they drained the monsters dry before the Kraken was able to finish the job? I guess we can hope that there are enough herbs, and the monsters fart so they're not harmed. But that's asking a lot of the monsters."

"No matter what," I said, "we need to make sure to tell all of the monsters to fart as much as they can if they're attacked. Then we won't even need herbs."

From the resort, we could hear the Nurses yell, "FAAAART! FAAAAART!"

"Looks like they already know," said Shane.

"But back to the Kraken," said Gordon. "What if he could take care of business even with the membranium's skin on?"

"It's too risky," I said. "We don't even know if we can control the Kraken. And the membranium will just get angrier and hungrier if we fail. We have to attack them when all of their skins are off. So, how do we get all of the skins off and keep them distracted?"

We all thought as hard as we could. It was hard with all the screaming.

"Wait!" yelled Ben. "I've got it! We just need to get Nabila out here."

"You're kidding, right?" said Gordon. "These guys are about to be sucked dry like a bowl of blood punch at a vampire prom, and all you can think about is your girlfriend?"

"She's not my girlfriend!" Ben yelled. "Hear me out! She showed us her machine that could make the sound of farting herring, right? If we could get her and her invention here, maybe she could attract a school of farting herring. She keeps the machine in her fanny pack, and she always has that on."

"But why would the membranium be interested in a school of farting herring?" I asked.

"We could wrangle the herring she attracts into a tank at the aquarium," Ben replied. "And then have the zombies bite all of them. Then, we'd have a school of zombified farting herring to lead down to the membranium hive with vegetable brain. We'd be able to lure ALL the skins *and* have a school of hungry fish to feast on the tender and delicious membranium organs!"

"Genius!" Shane yelled.

"All right," I said. "Let's tell Director Z and figure out how to get her here."

We all rushed back up to the resort. It was completely deserted. There was no steel drum music in the open-air theater. There was no zombie floating in the Jacuzzi.

"This is creepy," Ben said.

"If it wasn't for all of the screaming," Shane said, "I'd say that this place was abandoned."

We followed the screaming back to the infirmary.

"Oh man," Gordon said. "Look at that line."

A massive line had formed outside of the infirmary. It was filled with Nurses who each had a grip on a possessed old monster, waiting to get inside.

We ducked into the infirmary to see the Nurses and witches frantically running around, administering the herbal remedy to monsters that thrashed wildly. A few looked like they had farted successfully, and were calmly being checked out by Nurses. The others looked as if they were deep in the grip of membranium madness.

"Fart! Just fart as fast as you can!" yelled the swamp creature.

"Vhat do you mean?" croaked one weak-looking vampire. "I can't just faaaaaAAAARRGHHH!"

He writhed on his bed, went stiff as a board, and then farted.

"That's not the kind of fart we were hoping for," said Shane.

The vampire broke from his restraints, and grabbed the bag of herbs that was in the hand of the Nurse.

"These taste terrible!" yelled the vampire. "Let us eat in peace!"

He threw the bag of herbs in the fire that was built in the back of the infirmary to boil the cauldron. It burst into a purple flame.

The Nurse went to grab the vampire, but he jumped to the left and cackled wildly.

"We'll drain this one with one big slurp," the vampire yelled, and threw is head back. "Yummmmmmm . . ."

As the YUM went on, the vampire wrinkled up in front of our eyes. We could hear him being dried up and eaten, but there was nothing we could do.

"Disgusting!" said Gordon. "He looks mummified."

The skin crawled off the vampire, and he was left gasping for air. He let out one last death rattle and fell into the arms of the Nurse. The skin shot out of the room.

As the Nurse dragged him to the back of the infirmary, Shane said, "He's not the only one. Just look!"

The Nurse gently laid the vampire on top of a pile of poor, mummified monsters.

Director Z walked over to us.

"This isn't the safest place to be at the moment," he said. "Things are getting dire. We've cured a few thanks to the herbs, but it's been very hard to get the monsters to fart in time. And we can't keep this up forever."

"Well, no worries," Shane said, "because we've got an idea that's going to solve all of this."

"Let's go to my office, where it's safer," the Director said.

With the doors to Director Z's office closed, the screams of the monsters were almost drowned out.

Almost.

"What do you think, gentlemen?" said Director Z. "How are you going to save the day this time?"

"Zombie herring," said Ben. "We need you to get one of the girls who was with us on our school trip. How quickly can we make that happen?"

"I can call Ms. Veracruz straight away," said Director Z. "But, what do we need this girl for?"

"She has a device that can be used to call a school of herring," said Ben. "Did you know that herring fart—constantly, in fact? It's their way of communicating. We'll call a school, zombify them, and then use them to distract all of the membranium skin that's not already feasting on the monsters."

"And then what?" asked Director Z.

"And then," said Shane, "when the skinless membranium's organs are all squishy and juicy hanging out in the ocean, the school of herring will swarm . . . and feast!"

"Excellent!" said Director Z. "A wonderful idea!"

He picked up the phone, but frowned once it was up to his ear.

"The line is dead," he said.

He got up from behind his desk.

"I must find out who has cut the phone line, and see if it can be repaired," he said.

He stormed toward the door, which was thrown open in his face.

Griselda stood in the door with a crazy look in her eye, holding several long cords in her hand.

"Looking for something, Zachary dear?" she cackled.

"Griselda!" Director Z gasped.

"I'm afraid your dear Griselda is no longer here," said the twisted figure in the door. "And I'm afraid that you will not be getting off of this island! Welcome to your doom!"

A huge explosion rattled the resort.

"That sounds like the boat depot!" said Director Z.

In response, Griselda cackled and ran back into the resort.

"This has certainly changed things," said Director Z. "We've just lost our chief witch and herbalist at a time when we're already running out of herbal remedy, the phone lines have been cut, and we now have no boats to get off of the island."

Calling All Farters! Calling All Farters!

"Well, now," said Director Z, "we have to think of another plan—we can't summon your friend."

"What about Gil?" I asked. "Can he call the herring?"

"I don't think Gil is actually communicating when he farts," said Director Z. "I think he is simply . . . farting."

"All right," Ben said. "Stick me back in my sea worm. I want to go home."

"Wait!" said Gordon. "Maybe Ben's onto something. Let's just send a sea worm to get Nabila!"

"I'm afraid we can't do that," said Director Z. "The only woman who knows how to create the correct smellgood and hibernation spells is under the control of the membranium."

"But Nabila doesn't have a sense of smell," said Ben. "Would she be able to make the trip then?"

"Hmmm . . . ," said Director Z. "The trip will be long for her. She'll be confused and disoriented. However, the chances of her perishing inside of the worm are very slim."

"Let's do it, then!" I said.

"Does the intercom still work?" Director Z asked himself. He walked over to the door, and pressed a button on the box there. "Calling Nurse Kook."

There was a short pause.

"Yes, Boss?" Nurse Kook said over the intercom.

"Oh, good, the intercom still works!" said Director Z. "Please send the swiftest sea worm over to my office, immediately."

"Your office?" asked Nurse Kook.

"Immediately," replied Director Z.

There was another pause. We listened to the crackle of the intercom and screams in the distance.

"Okay, Boss," said Nurse Kook. "Sea worm's on its way to you."

"How are things at the aquarium?" asked Director Z. "Have you had any problems guarding it?"

"So far, so good, Boss," said Nurse Kook. "Everyone seems to be fine here."

"Excellent!" said Director Z. "It looks like the membranium either can't get through the filtration system of the tanks, or are unaware of the aquatic residents. Thank you, Nurse Kook."

Director Z returned to his desk. Just as he sat down, there was a crash, and a sea worm head burst through the window.

"Oh, man!" said Gordon. "Not that smell again!"

"Ah," said Director Z to the sea worm. "Thank you for being so quick. We need you to head back to Cape Canaveral, as swiftly as you can."

The sea worm nodded its slimy head. Director Z turned to us.

"Whom does the sea worm seek?" he asked.

"Her name is Nabila," said Ben. "She's small with dark, beautiful eyes and—"

"Actually," I said, "she's really easy to find. She has the thickest glasses and the shiniest braces you've ever seen."

"You forgot the fanny pack," added Shane. "It's hot pink."

"Seek the bespectacled but beautiful bearer of the fluorescent fanny pack," boomed Director Z. "Be discreet. But most of all, be swift. And drop this message off with Ms. Veracruz. You will know her by her hairnet."

Director Z scribbled on a piece of paper and held it up. The sea worm slurped it up, leaving a bit of slime on his hand.

"What are you telling her?" asked Shane.

“To prepare more memory-erasing serum,” Director Z replied.

The sea worm backed out of the window. When his head had fully cleared, the frame fell into the office with a CLUNK, and the stinky, cool air was replaced with fresh, warm air.

Director Z stuck his head out of the window, and called to the exiting sea worm.

“NEXT TIME, PLEASE USE THE DOOR!”

As the sun rose on Paradise Island, the situation had gone from bad to insane. We had gone over every detail of our plan twenty times, and all we needed now was for Nabila to arrive. We waited on the beach for her sea worm to come in. Ben, more nervous than usual, paced across the sand.

From behind us, the sound of broken glass filled the air. We turned our heads to see a monster sailing from the top floor of the resort.

“It looks like the membranium have figured out how to get into the rooms,” I said.

“At least the skin will protect him from the fall,” added Shane. “That’s one positive thing.”

“Why are we just sitting here waiting!?” groaned

Gordon. "I could be up there shoving herbs into monster mouths!"

He kicked a mound of sand.

"There aren't many herbs left," said Shane. "It's safest for us down here at the beach, and we need to be here when Nabila arrives, or she's going to be crazy confused."

"Gordon's right, though," I said. "We shouldn't *all* be down here. It's insane up at the resort! Sure, we saved a dozen monsters, but most of them are so weak they can't even help with the superpowered skin on. The dead monster pile was pretty deep when we left."

"Director Z is in control for now," said Ben. "We just have to hope he stays in control. Once the herbs run out, the membranium will drain the monsters *fast*!"

More membranium skin shimmied up the shore.

"Hurrrryyyyy!" I yelled out into the ocean.

As if in response, the sea worm crashed out of the ocean, and crawled up to the beach.

WHAAARRRFFF!

It barfed up Nabila, and then backed down into the water. We ran up to her with the towels we had brought, and surrounded her.

"Oh, man!" said Ben, waving a hand around in front of his face. "I can't imagine how bad that would have smelled."

She was curled up in a pile of goo, and we bent down

to clean her off. Shane reached to roll her over onto her back, and she sprang up in one fast jump.

"Aaaarrrrgh!" she yelled, and whipped something out of her fanny pack.

There was a crackle and Shane jumped back.

"It's a Taser!" Gordon yelled, and rushed at her.

"WAAAAAIT!" I yelled.

Everybody stopped.

"What. Is. Going. ON?" Nabila asked. She gripped the Taser, which was still crackling loudly.

"Nabila," I said. "We need your help with the . . ."

I hesitated, but then continued. "With the old monsters from Raven Hill. They're here on vacation."

She looked confused for a few seconds, and then she put the Taser back into her fanny pack.

"Oh, wow," she said. "This is AMAZING!"

She looked down at her clothes, which were still covered in sand and sea worm gunk.

"Was that a giant sea worm?" she asked. "It was so tight in there, I passed out after a few hours."

"We didn't mean to startle you," said Ben. "But it was the only way we could get you here quickly. Luckily for you, you can't smell. Those things smell terrible."

"Wait," she said, looking confused again, "how do you know I don't have a sense of smell? How do you even know my name? I was going to introduce myself on the science trip, but you guys didn't join us."

“Well, it’s a long story and we don’t have much time,” I said, “but the short story is that you DID meet us on the trip to Cape Canaveral. Then, on the first night, *we* got taken away in sea worms to here: Paradise Island. You, and all the other students were given a memory-erasing serum to forget us.”

“I thought breakfast that first morning tasted unusual,” she said.

“What we really need to know,” said Ben, “is if you have that fish-calling device in your fanny pack. We need your help to attract a group of farting herring, zombify them, and use them to lure the skin off a disgusting hive of sea creatures called the membranium.”

“Wow, this is unbelievable. Yes, I’ve got it!” she said. “I’ve never tested the farting herring setting, but many of the others function well.”

“Great,” I said. “We have to work quickly—we don’t have that much more time. Let me introduce you to—”

“Director Z?” she asked.

“Yep,” said Shane. “It doesn’t look like you forgot anything you heard us say at lunch!”

“We’ll fill you in on the way up to Director Z’s office,” I said.

As we headed up the trail, the screams got louder and louder.

We stood in front of the door to Director Z's office.

"And that's why we need the farting herring," Ben finished explaining, with a smile.

"And why they need to be zombified," she said, and she smiled back. "Got it. I'm ready."

They stared into each other's eyes, grinning ear to ear.

"Great," I said, and shook her hand to break up the staring contest. "Welcome to the club. I'm really sorry about before."

"Before?" she asked.

"Never mind," Gordon said.

Gordon lifted his clenched fist to the door, about to knock, when . . .

WHOOOSH!

It swung open. A crazy-looking Director Z nearly knocked us over as he breezed past.

"Hey," I yelled. "Hold on a minute!"

He turned awkwardly in the hallway—first his head, and then his body.

He looked at us with a crooked grin for a moment, and then finally said, "Oh! Gentlemen! Just who I was looking for."

He clapped his hands together and shuffled us into the office. He closed the door behind him.

"Please, gentlemen," he said. "Have a seat. And who is your new friend?"

He sat down and put his feet up on his desk.

"This is—" Gordon started, but I cut him off.

"New? Nabila's been with us from the start," I said.

"Oh," Director Z's eyes searched the room, looking confused, but that same crooked grin stayed on his face. "Of course! Nabila. I'm so sorry, I've been quite busy fighting the membranium."

"Wait," she started to say, "I just—"

"—have been having a great time in the tropics?" asked Shane. "Us, too. In fact, let's hit the beach!"

Shane got up, and everyone followed. Everyone but Nabila.

"What is going on here?" Nabila asked. "I thought I had just figured everything out . . ."

Nabila was so confused, her eyebrows formed a *V*.

"Yes," said Director Z, "I would like to know the very same thing. What *is* going on here? I seem to remember us talking about a plan? Chris, you are my number one. Always by my side. I'm sure you remember us talking about it."

"Yeah," I said. "We're still planning to hike through the jungle tomorrow. Five a.m. Don't be late."

"Come on, Nabila," said Ben, and then in a whisper, *"Please!"*

She looked at him strangely, but got up.

We all headed to the door.

"WAIT," boomed Director Z. "ALL OF YOU WAIT."

RUN!!!

We turned around. Director Z was no longer smiling. His body was bent over slightly, and his face was red with anger.

"We're through being nice," he hissed.

"Leave these monsters alone!" I yelled.

"You might as well tell a lion to stop eating a gazelle," Evil Z growled. "We must feast. And feast we will."

"But why the monsters?" I asked as we backed toward the door. "Why now?"

"It is their will," Evil Z replied. "We must collect all the juice. And in return, we shall rule all the seas of the Earth."

"Not if we can help it," I said, and turned the doorknob.

It wouldn't budge.

"Looking for this?" Evil Z hissed, and held up a key.

"What is he doing?" screamed Nabila.

"The membranium have taken him over," Ben replied.

"Indeed we have," said Evil Z. "And if you tell me what I want to know, I just may spare you scrawny children. WHAT IS THE PLAN?"

"Plan?" Shane scoffed. "Plan!? Director Z has just spent the last day saying how you guys are completely invincible."

"Nice try," said Evil Z, "but we have tapped his mind, and know there is a plan to stop us. We just don't know what that plan is. But you're going to tell us."

"All right, you win," said Shane. "I'll tell you everything you want to know."

"Dude!" protested Gordon.

Shane walked over toward the desk, and stood between the leather couch and the broken fish tank.

"Where should we start?" asked Shane.

Evil Z came out from behind his desk, and stood between Shane and the fish tank.

"Very good, very good," said Evil Z. "We are very, very pleased that you've decided to tell us the plan. We will crush those lumbering Nurses!"

"Get ready for the plan," said Shane.

He turned his head back to us, winked, and then

turned back to Evil Z who was wringing his hands together.

"I dunno what Shane's doing," I whispered to the others, "but we should get ready."

"The plan is simple, really," said Shane. "I'm going to deliver a powerful roundhouse kick to your head, you'll fall back into the fish tank and get snagged by the razor coral and broken glass, and then, rather than waste time looking for the key in your pocket and exiting from the front door, we'll all jump out of the window."

"What?" screamed Evil Z. "How dare you sass us, you impudent little fool!"

Evil Z rushed at Shane, who landed a roundhouse kick square in his jaw. Evil Z flew back onto the fish tank with a crunch.

"Run!!!" I yelled, and we all rushed for the window.

"Arrrrgggh!" Evil Z yelled.

He tried to pull himself out of the fish tank, and though there was a loud RIP, his clothes stayed snagged by the coral that was secured inside.

"NOOOOOOO!" he struggled.

More tearing and screaming could be heard as we each jumped a few feet down onto the ground and ran for the aquarium.

"Let's hope that he stays stuck for long enough," I said.

We were out of breath when we hit the aquarium a few minutes later. Nurse Kook had sealed himself into the entrance. We ran up to the huge metal blockade and knocked as hard as we could. A few moments later, a door in the metal scraped to the side, and we were let in.

"The Director has been taken over," Gordon said to Nurse Kook. "We have to work quickly!"

We rushed over to a pile of scuba gear, and Nurse Kook helped us put it on.

We ran up to the top of an empty tank that was open to the ocean. Two old zombies waited for us there.

"Are you guys ready?" I asked them.

They each gave me a big thumbs-up, although one of them was missing a thumb.

"All right," I said. "Everyone take some of Griselda's gas elixir. Be careful, this is all that's left."

We each whipped out a vial that was in a small pouch on our wet suits.

"Ach," said Ben. "This tastes terrible! Are you sure it's not barf elixir?"

"Don't fart it all out at once," said Shane.

"Nabila, you know what to do!" I said.

"Got it!" she said.

She switched on the little black device she held in her hand.

PLIP, PLIP, PLIP, PLIP!

"Those don't sound like farts," said Gordon. "Are

you sure we shouldn't use mine?"

"I assure you," said Nabila, "that this is the actual sound of herring farts. Underwater farts sound different, you know."

She lowered her device into the tank.

FLURT, FLURT, FLURT, FLURT, FLURT!

"Ah," said Shane. "That's more like it."

"Now we wait," said Nabila.

We waited, and waited, and waited. Five minutes went by and it felt like five years.

"What if this doesn't work?" whined Ben.

"It has to work," said Gordon, "we don't have a Plan B."

"I really wish that Gil could speak Herring," said Shane.

"I'm starting to worry. I'm sure Evil Z has freed himself by now," I said. "And this tank is wide open! What if the skin is attracted to the farting?"

The water began to bubble and froth at the entrance of the tank.

"The herring!" Nabila yelled.

"YES!" I yelled.

Nabila's machine slowly drew the massive school of herring over to where we stood. The zombies shuffled over in preparation.

When they reached the edge of the tank, the four of us threw a large net over the herring, and jumped into the water.

As soon as we hit the water we could hear millions of tiny farts a second.

FLURT, FLURT, FLURT, FLURT, FLURT.

"Take it slow," I said through the radio communicator, "we don't want to spook them."

"The school is massive," said Shane. "There must be a thousand fish in there!"

"This is awesome!" Nabila said. "They're actually wolf herring, so they have loads of teeth. Farewell, organs!"

"All right," I said. "Let's pull the bottom of the net up so we can let the zombies in."

We got the net right where we wanted it, and I came up to the surface of the water to call the zombies . . .

. . . only to find Evil Z standing in a badly-shredded suit at the edge of the tank!

"Hello, children," he growled.

SWIM!!!

“We are very, very disappointed in you,” said Evil Z. “But, in the end, your plan is of no consequence to us. You will be defeated, you weak little babies!!!”

He walked to the wall at the back of the tank platform and hit a large red button. An alarm sounded, and red lights flashed.

My friends surfaced around me.

“What’s going on?” asked Ben.

I pointed at Evil Z, who approached the water’s edge again.

“We have let all the sea monsters loose,” cackled Evil Z. “If they don’t get you—we will!”

He grabbed both zombies by the arm and turned to leave.

"Wait!" I yelled. "Whatever you do, please don't hurt them!"

"Oh," said Evil Z, "are these two juicy tidbits important to you? Then watch them DIE!"

He tossed the two zombies into the water and stormed off the platform.

"There's plenty of food back at the facility," he said, "and now WE'RE IN CONTROL. HA-HA-HA-HA! Let the feast begin!"

Evil Z stormed through the door to the main hall of the aquarium and locked us inside.

The zombies dog-paddled slowly toward me. The tank was soon filled with angry growls.

"The sea monsters!" Gordon yelled.

"Chris, get those zombies chompin'," Shane said. "I think I can give you some time, but I don't know how much, so HURRY!"

Shane dipped under the water and swam off.

"Wait!" I yelled, and ducked underwater to see where he was going. "Shane, what are you doing?"

"The Kraken," he said back. "I've got to get the Kraken—"

With a burst of static, his transmission cut off.

"Shane? Shane!?" I yelled into the communicator. "Argh! Guys—let's do this! Hold the netting tight."

I swam over to the struggling zombies, grabbed each by the arm, and brought them over to the opening in the net the others had created.

They leaned in and CHOMPED into a few herring.

CHOMP, CHOMP, CHOMP!

Soon, the zombie's chomps were joined by smaller chomps.

"The first zombie herring are starting to bite the others," said Ben.

"That's good, guys," I said to the zombies.

They turned to slowly dog-paddle back to the platform. I swam ahead of them to get the vegetable brain.

Suddenly, one of them splashed in the water.

"Arrrrgggbbbbbwww!" he screamed into the water.

"Oh, no," said Ben. "A membranium!"

"Let's get these fish moving, now!" yelled Gordon.

"We can't yet!" I yelled. "We need the vegetable brain to lead them in the right direction."

I shot out of the water, and grabbed the platform edge.

The zombie under attack knocked me back in the water before I could grab the vegetable brain. He splashed around so violently I was pinned between him and the wall.

"He's right on top of you," yelled Ben. "Unless he farts, the membranium will grab you as soon as they have control. TELL HIM TO FART!"

"OOF," I grunted as a zombie arm smashed into my stomach.

"I'm not taking any chances," said Nabila.

She broke away from her position at the net and swam toward me and the writhing zombie—backward!

"What are you doing?" screamed Ben.

"Trust me," she said.

She backed her backside right up against the writhing zombie and

PLRFFFTTTTTTTT!

He stopped writhing.

"Get back!" yelled Gordon. "The membranium just squeezed him."

"Oh, no it didn't," she said.

The zombie began swimming up to the platform, faster now. I quickly helped him up and then grabbed the vegetable brain. Nabila helped the second zombie up and we headed back to the net.

"Did you just fart on him?" I asked.

"Yes," she said. "In fact, I did."

"Wait," said Gordon. "That works?"

Ben stared at his not-girlfriend in complete admiration.

"Wow," I said. "This girl is AWESOME!"

"Thanks, guys," said Nabila, "but let's get going."

I headed to the front of the net and waved the

vegetable brain in front of the herring. They slowly started to move forward.

"Nabila and Gordon," I said, "grab hold of the net just in case the zombie herring get any funny ideas. I want you to be able to put them back on the right course."

"Got it," said Nabila.

"Ben," I continued, "keep an eye out for membranium and sea monsters.

FURT, FLURT, FURT, PLURT, FUURT!

The zombie herring happily farted their way into the deep, following the vegetable brain. They picked up speed, but when we passed over the coral reef, they got a little distracted by some of the tastier sea creatures.

"Maybe they can smell fish brains?" Gordon wondered.

We reached the lip of the trench down to the membranium hive.

"Oh no," said Ben. "We can't get down there!"

The dark figure of Moby Dick, the monstrous white whale, loomed at the edge of the trench. He was soon joined by dozens of slimy sea serpents. Razor sharp teeth shined in the water.

We froze in place.

"What do we do?" screamed Nabila. "Never mind; I don't want to meet any more monsters! This is more than enough."

"Pull yourself together, Nabila!" I yelled.

But I was just as frightened as Nabila. Even the zombie fish were stunned.

With a great blast of snotty bubbles from Moby Dick, the sea monsters headed straight toward us.

"Back up, back up!" I yelled.

I swung around to the other side of the net, and waved the vegetable brain around like crazy.

But it was too late.

The sea monsters rose out of the trench, and surrounded us.

FAAAAART!!!

Great roars, squeals and moans sounded in the deep. Mouths filled with razor-sharp teeth snapped. A hydra moved closer, each head looking straight into each of our eyes. Moby Dick opened his mouth wide and . . .

"Yahhoooooooo!"

There was a scream and a huge dark figure swooped in from above us.

"It's the Kraken," yelled Ben.

"Look." Nabila pointed.

On top of the Kraken's head, holding on like a crazed bull rider, was Shane.

"Yeeeeeeehaw!" Shane yelled. "Catch us if you can!"

The Kraken turned back the way it came, and the sea monsters sped in its direction.

"Awesome!" said Ben. "Yeah, Shane!"

"Ben!" yelled Nabila. "Look out!"

One last sea serpent roared past us, smacking Ben in the head as it went. Ben was flung down onto the sea floor. With an OOF, his oxygen tanks crunched into the sharp coral.

"Are you okay?" Nabila squealed.

"I'm. S-so. D-dizzy," stammered Ben.

"That's all right, beautiful one," a voice shimmered in the deep.

"We'll take care of you," said another, equally magical voice.

"Whoa," said Gordon. "Mermaids!"

"Oh, I don't think so," said Nabila.

She swam down to Ben and grabbed one of his arms just as another was grabbed by the mermaid.

"I've got him," said Nabila.

"Oh, but my dear, we're more than capable of taking care of him," a mermaid purred.

"I said *I've* got him," growled Nabila.

"It's okay," said Ben. "Let me go with the pretty mermaid."

"What?" gasped Nabila and let him go.

"Oh, you're such a cute little one," said another mermaid. "We're going to have so much fun."

The mermaids swam off with Ben.

"He's MY cute one," yelled Nabila, and followed the exiting mermaids.

"Nabila," I yelled. "NABILA! We don't have much time now. I'm sure Ben will be fine with the mermaids. But we need you. Gordon and I can't do this alone."

Nabila turned around.

"Fine," she said. "Ben can take care of himself. I'm ready."

I moved the back over the trench with the vegetable brain. We had just picked up speed again when . . .

"Chris," Gordon yelled. "Look out! To your right!"

I turned just in time to see the shimmer of skin as it quickly enveloped me from head to toe.

"Arrrrgggh!" I yelled.

It was surprisingly fast, and surprisingly strong. Every single inch of me was squeezed. Pain flashed like lightning in my eyes. My brain felt like it was being taken over, and words rushed into my head and made me dizzy.

You are ours now! Submit! Open your mind to us!

"Fart!" yelled Nabila, and I snapped out of it.

I was in so much pain, I was barely able to do it, but I finally let out a BLLLLURP.

"Whoa!" I yelled, catching my breath.

"Faaaarrt!" yelled Gordon.

"I just did!" I yelled back.

"No, you didn't," Gordon said. "All you did was yell, 'Cheesecake whoa!'"

But I must have farted. I could still feel the skin on me, but it was no longer pressing me. In fact, it made me feel even stronger.

"No, he farted," said Nabila. "Now, let's hurry up and get down there so we can get out of here."

I went over the side of the ridge into the darkness. The farting zombie herring followed.

Two more skins shimmered past.

"Look out!" I yelled, but soon Nabila and Gordon were thrashing and dealing with the insane pain.

"Fart, fart, faaaart!" I yelled so hard that my ears hurt inside my scuba gear.

BLLLLLAARRRP!

"Easy-peasy lemon squeezy," said Gordon, coughing.

"Fart, Gordon!" I yelled. "Fart!"

"He farted," said Nabila.

"No, he didn't," I said. "He just said—"

"We can talk about it later," said Gordon, pointing forward.

We had arrived at the hive.

"We need one last push to get these herring into the hive," I said.

"Got it," they said.

"This is it, guys!" I said.

"Let's do it!" said Gordon.

I swam ahead with the vegetable brain, while Nabila and Gordon grabbed the top of the net, and the first of the zombie herring made their way out.

"Build up some speed, guys," I yelled.

We all kicked as hard as we could.

"All right," I yelled. "I'm letting go of the vegetable brain in three . . . two . . . one . . . GO!"

I flung the brain into the hive and swam back toward Nabila and Gordon. They slowly peeled the net off the school and headed back up toward the ridge. As I swam past the school, there was a shimmer of skin, and three zombie herring were suddenly wrapped around me.

"AHHHH!" I shrieked.

They chomped my body like crazy, and it sounded like they were farting directly into my ears.

"Chris!" Gordon yelled, and he began to swim back toward me.

"Wait," I said. "The skin I have on is protecting me. Let's get out of here."

I swam toward Gordon and away from the hive, which awoke with the appearance of the zombie herring.

But soon I was being pulled backward! The zombie herring had created a layer of fart under the skin, and were no longer pressed against my body. They headed back to the school.

"Chris!" yelled Nabila.

"Forget it!" I yelled back. "Just go!"

I turned around and saw the school follow the vegetable brain into the very center of the hive. The membranium came a little farther out of their sea pods, hissing and growling in excitement at their tasty new visitors. Their moldy claws cracked, and they drooled a blue cloud out of the sides of their mouths. Their tongues lashed behind their razor-sharp shark teeth.

This better work, I thought, *or I'll be membranium meat.*

Slowly, disgustingly, all of the membranium peeled off their skins like slimy T-shirts. The ocean was filled with a wet, tearing sound, as hundreds of nasty, green, scaly skins peeled off of ugly bodies, and turned clear as they headed for the fish.

FURT, PLURT, FLART, PLIP, PLOP!

The herring farted as the skin overtook them.

"It's working!" I yelled. "Go, guys, goooooo!"

"All right, all right," said Gordon, "but keep us updated with the communicator. We're going to try to find Shane and the Kraken. Maybe they can help."

Entire walls of membranium were now exposed, their organs pulsating in the cold water, giving off heat waves.

"The herring have noticed the organs," I yelled.

A few of the herring had broken off from the rest, and were chomping at the organs of the membranium. Soon they were thrashing, which got the others' attentions.

"It's a feeding frenzy!" I said.

My three zombie herring brought me up against the wall to join the feast, and I was pulled in all sorts of different directions, scraping up against the wall and squishing into sea pods.

The sounds of scraping and squishing mixed with the bloodcurdling screams of the membranium as they were devoured.

The water began to cloud with blood as organs were chewed up in seconds. Entire walls of the hideous beasts were taken down by the frantic fish, who were farting even faster and stronger now.

"I'm getting pummeled by all of the fish," I said. "They're not hurting me, but I'm dizzy, and—"

My helmet was knocked off the side of my head, with a large scrape, as we bounced off the wall and joined the rest of the school.

"Chris," Nabila said, "can you hear us? Chris?"

I held my breath, struggling to put my helmet back on. Meanwhile, the three zombie herring trapped in our bubble started chewing into anything they could, still hungry after all of the tasty organs.

"Chris?" asked Gordon.

I finally got my helmet on and then CHOMP, one of the zombie herring bit into the air hose feeding my helmet.

"Uh, oh," I said. "Oh . . ."

I gagged on the next breath. The bubble of skin

expanded with the green and brown gas of the zombie herring that were trapped with me.

"Oh, it's terrible," I said.

"What's going on down there?" asked Gordon.

"My skin. Is filling up. With gas," I said between coughs.

Sure enough, the entire school was slowly becoming separated as bubbles of gas formed in what used to be the membranium skin. And I was in the middle of it all.

"We're coming down there," said Gordon.

I coughed and gagged. It smelled a million times worse than being trapped under a sheet with Gordon's fart.

The herring, frightened by being trapped in their own gas, began farting even harder. We started to rise in the water, slowly at first, and then picking up speed as the bubbles expanded even further.

The bubble I was in popped with a loud BANG. We jiggled the hundreds of other bubbles, most of which were filled by one or two fish.

"No!" I yelled, still coughing in the green/brown fart stew. "Turn back!"

COUGH, GAG, COUGH!

"The skins," I screamed between coughs, "ARE GOING TO EXPLODE!"

But it was too late. The gas bubbles were expanding at amazing rates, and the frantic school rose up the side of the trench.

The entire mass of bubbles began to jiggle and vibrate, until, suddenly.

POW! POP! BAM! BLORP!

All the bubbles burst violently and shot us to the surface of the water. I flew up out of the water fifteen feet and then landed on top of a huge wave that had formed by the explosion. It crashed over the beach, over the jungle, and smashed into the resort!

When I finally stopped spinning, I found myself facedown in the Jacuzzi!

Gordon and a mermaid washed up nearby, in the infinity pool. I scanned the horizon for Ben, Nabila, and Shane, but all I could see were zombie herring flip-flopping everywhere. A few wet Nurses looked around confused, and waved their hands at the horrendous odor that had washed up with the wave.

"Do you see the others?" I asked Gordon.

"Ben and Nabila, sitting in a tree . . . ," Gordon said, and pointed up.

"Just so you know, we are NOT k-i-s-s-i-n-g," came Nabila's voice from above.

I looked up to see Ben and Nabila tangled up in the fronds of a palm tree.

"Woooo-hooo," Ben yelled. "And I didn't even barf in my helmet!"

Gordon turned to the mermaid in the pool.

"So," he cooed, "what are you doing later?"

The Sweet Stench of Success

I laid in the Jacuzzi for a few minutes, and let the bubbles blurp at my backside.

"Ahhh," I sighed.

"Can someone get me out of here?" asked Ben from his perch.

"Relax and enjoy the view," scolded Nabila. "Or are you still trying to get away from me?"

"No, I'm not. But, how can you enjoy the view, when—oh, riiiiiiight," said Ben. "You can't smell the massive fartbomb that just exploded."

A zombie herring flopped out of the palm tree above Ben and smacked him in the head on its way down.

"I think it smells like victory!" said Shane, who ran up to the infinity pool and jumped in.

"I don't want to know what losing smells like," quipped Gordon, floating in the pool.

"Shane!" I yelled. "How were you able to ride the Kraken? That was amazing!"

"I just remember what Gordon told me Clive had said," Shane said. "And gave him one swift karate chop to the top of his head."

"Works every time, brah," a weak voice came from the pool.

"Hey, what's that?" Gordon said.

I lifted my head out of the relaxing Jacuzzi and looked to see Gordon pointing to something bobbing up and down in the water.

"Is that Clive?" Gordon asked.

"WHAT!?" I yelled, and jumped out of the Jacuzzi.

Shane ducked underwater, and swam up to the surface a few seconds later with . . .

"CLIVE!" I yelled. "You're alive! I mean, you're not dead. I mean . . . it's great to see you!"

Shane lifted him up to the side of the pool, and I dragged out the old zombie surfer.

"Hey, buddy," he gurgled, water pouring out of his mouth. "I think I'm a little waterlogged here. Get me in some sun!"

"What happened?" I asked. "I thought we lost you!"

Shane walked over to Clive and me. Gordon swam up to the side of the pool. Ben waved from the palm tree.

"Hey, I think I tweaked my right ear," Clive said. "Is it still there?"

I turned his head to have a look, and a crab scurried out of his ear and into the jungle.

"I think it's fine now," Shane said. "So, what happened?"

"Well, I was able to hide in a small crevice under the coral where the sharks couldn't reach me," he said, "but when they finally left, I realized I was stuck. How did I get here?"

"It's a long story," I said, "but the short version is—"

Before I could start, Director Z, a dozen Nurses, and almost all of the residents showed up poolside. Some of them looked like they were about to fall over, and were held up by other residents, or by the Nurses.

"Chris," said Director Z, "you and your friends have done it again! I'm so very, very pleased."

The crowd burst into applause, the monsters laughing and smiling.

"Aw, thanks!" I said. "We had a lot of help. Gil, your farts are amazing! Clive, you saved our lives! And, Nabila! We never could have done it without you."

The swamp creature walked out of the crowd and I gave him such a hard hug that he farted . . . of course! Then I shook the Director's hand.

"Don't forget to thank Ms. Veracruz," said Director Z. "If it weren't for the rare zombie piranha she fed you, you wouldn't have been quite so agile in the water."

"Zombie," Gordon choked, "piranha?"

A shower of vomit fell from the palm tree. Poor Ben.

"Yes, twice actually," Director Z said. "Once at school—"

"The Mac 'n' Sneeze!" Shane yelled. "I *knew* it tasted fishy!"

"And again during the barbecue in Cape Canaveral," finished Director Z.

"Aw, man," said Gordon, "my stomach is cramping."

Gordon grunted and little bubbles rose to the surface of the pool. As each one popped we heard:

"POP—Oh—POP—man—POP—I—POP—ate—PLIP—zombie—PLUP—piranha!"

"Interesting," Director Z said. "The zombie piranha was meant to help you swim faster in case you ended up in the water. But apparently, a side effect is that you can fartspeak."

Shane lifted his leg and farted a single word: "AWESOME."

"Everyone that still has skin on them is fine," Director Z said, "although they no longer have superstrength. If it wasn't for that superstrength, I don't think we would have made it through the day. I'm told a werewolf and Gil personally held me down to keep me from wreaking havoc on the facility. I want to apologize for my actions. I couldn't fight the mind control."

"It wasn't your fault," said Shane, "but I apologize for kicking you in the noggin."

"Not a problem," said Director Z, rubbing his jaw. "Now, how do we get out of this skin? Any ideas?"

"Get to fartin'!" said Gordon. "You've got to pop it like a balloon!"

"That's what caused the fartsunami," I said. "All the zombie herring popped their skin bubbles at once."

"Fartsunami!" Ben called down from the palm tree. "That's awesome!"

"Well, it looks like we have a lot to fartspeak about," said Director Z.

Shane looked at Director Z strangely.

"I ate zombie piranha as well," Director Z said.

"Ohhhhhhh," we all said.

Grigore walked forward and stood next to the swamp creature.

"Chris," said Grigore, "I just vant to apologize on behalf of all the residents. You saved us from the sussuroblats, cleaned up our messes, wiped blood soup off our mouths, made our coffins, and ve returned the favor by treating you like servants. Ve're very sorry—ve've not quite been ourselves. Ve vere cooped up and getting crazy in Raven Hill. It vas hard *not* to be cranky. But ve'll try to be better. Ve'll try our best to vork as a team."

"Hear, hear!" screamed the crowd.

"Now," yelled Director Z, "let's soak up some sun, eat a few zombie frogs, relax, and build up our lebensplasm!"

Gordon jumped out of the pool and walked over to Director Z.

"I was just wondering if I could ask you one thing," said Gordon.

"Please," said Director Z, "anything you need."

"Can you just call it *monster juice*? It sounds so much more fun than lebensplasm."

"MONSTER JUICE!" yelled Clive from his seat.

"All right," said Director Z, "*monster juice* it is!"

The crowd cheered.

We spent the next few days at Paradise Island, enjoying the sun, sand, and sea. The swamp creature and I took a trip down to the membranium hive to make sure it was completely destroyed. It was. Clive gave us surfing lessons. Shane finally got his fruit smoothie. And when the zombie sharks returned to the aquarium, we made them special vegetable-brain smoothies.

It was the vacation we had desperately needed.

A Nurse fixed the telephone lines and we called in transportation. We returned to Cape Canaveral, where Lunch Lady made all the preparations for folks to think we had been there the whole time.

Then it was back home!

I walked into my house completely relaxed, but before I could say, “Hello,” my mother attacked me.

“Chrissy!” she screeched. “You have A LOT of explaining to do!”

“Huh?” I asked. “What’s going on?”

“THAT’S WHAT I WANT TO KNOW!” she screeched even louder.

“Whoa, Mom,” I said, “calm down.”

“I will not calm down!” she said. “I can’t even count how many times I called you, and you never called back! You always call back! What’s going on?”

“I was just hanging out with my friends,” I replied.

“Oh, really?” she asked. “I saw all sorts of pictures from parents of their kids, and you’re not in any of them. We always talk about how much you love space, and you didn’t even text me a photo of Kennedy Space Center!”

“Mom, I was busy,” I said, starting to get nervous.

What if she knows about my trip to Paradise Island? I wondered.

“Yeah, you’re always busy these days,” she replied. “Ever since you started volunteering at Raven Hill, you’ve been so busy . . . and acting so *strange*.”

“It’s . . . hard work,” I stammered. “Really tiring. Sorry if I’m a little out of it and just wanted to relax on vacation.”

“Chris, I know you too well. Something’s wrong. What’s going on at Raven Hill? You always stay there so late. I’ve been e-mailing your father about it, and he’s just as worried.”

“All right, Mom, all right!” I said, not really knowing what to say. “Everything is fine. Nothing is wrong.”

“I think it’s about time I spoke with the Director of Raven Hill,” she said. “In fact, I think I would like to speak with him IMMEDIATELY. RIGHT NOW.”

“All right,” I said, not knowing what to do. “I guess I’ll go and get him.”

“Go and get him?” Mom said. “I don’t want you go anywhere until I speak with him—just give me his number.”

“I . . . don’t have his number,” I said.

“Well,” she said, grabbing her purse, “I’ll go up there myself.”

“No, wait,” I said. “Everything’s fine, and there’s nothing to worry about. I need . . . um . . . I need to get my volunteer form anyway! Trust me.”

“FINE,” she yelled. “But if you come back here without the Director, you’re going to be sorry.”

I biked up to Raven Hill as quickly as I could. My

mind was buzzing. *What are we going to tell my mother? We have to tell her something!*

But soon my mind was buzzing even more. When I reached the top of the hill, there was nothing there but a smoldering pile of rubble. The Nurses were erecting large tents behind the burned remains of Raven Hill. Director Z stood in front of the building with his head down.

"Director Z!" I yelled. "What happened?"

"Chris!" he replied. "It's terrible. The ravens—and there are only three of them now—report that Herr Direktor Detlef was a tool of the membranium this whole time. He never intended to bring his residents to Raven Hill. They were all sucked dry by the membranium shortly before we arrived. We were lured to Paradise Island by the membranium! Herr Direktor Detlef destroyed our facility—and himself."

He paused, then said, quietly, "There's something bigger going on here. Why would the membranium want to destroy Raven Hill?"

"When you were possessed," I said, "you said that someone was making the membranium collect all the monster juice."

"Yes, I seem to remember that now . . . ," said Director Z. "And 'they' look to be collecting even more than monster juice. Herr Direktor Detlef's pendant can't be found anywhere."

"Pendant?" I asked.

Director Z loosened his tie and pulled a necklace out from under his shirt. A sliver of bloodstone hung off the bottom.

"Every Director has one, and Herr Direktor Detlef's is gone. This is all very troubling," said the Director.

A Nurse approached with a slightly-charred painting. He held it up to Director Z.

"I told you so," said Lucinda B. Smythe.

The Nurse carried the painting away.

"What are you going to do?" I asked.

"We don't have the resources to rebuild," he said, sadly. "So we'll have to seek shelter somewhere else. I'm not sure where yet."

"Well," I said, "we have another problem."

"What?" he said.

"My mother knows something's going on at Raven Hill."

"We'll just have the witches whip up a batch of memory-erasing serum."

"No, it's not that simple. My father's in Afghanistan with the Air Force Reserve, and she's already e-mailed him about it. We can't erase his memory—unless you have a facility in Afghanistan, and can find him. His mission is classified—but there are e-mail records, and the US government doesn't destroy e-mail records. She's asked to speak with you right away."

"All right." He sighed.

We both looked at the smoldering rubble, and at the same time, said:

"We should have just stayed on Paradise Island."

About the Author . . .

M. D. Payne is a mad scientist who creates monsters by stitching together words instead of dead body parts. After nearly a decade in multimedia production for public radio, he entered children's publishing as a copywriter and marketer. Monster Juice is his debut series. He lives in the tiny village of New York City with his wife and baby girl, and hopes to add a hairy, four-legged monster to his family soon.